SAVY
WISDOM 2

The Sequel

By
New York Times Best-Selling Author
Peggy McColl

Hasmark
PUBLISHING
INTERNATIONAL

ISBN-13: 978-1-77482-138-1

ISBN-10: 1774821389

Published by:

Hasmark Publishing International

Important Disclaimers

The author has done their best to present accurate and up-to-date information in this book but cannot guarantee that the information is correct or will suit your particular situation. Further, the publisher has used its best efforts in preparing this book, and the information provided herein is provided "as is."

We can't guarantee any results from the use of our programs or any of the information contained in this book, though we genuinely believe that this information will help you reach your goals. Like with any program, your results are limited by your willingness to take action as well as factors outside of your control and our control. By reading this book and enrolling in any programs you hereby understand the potential risks when embarking upon a goal achievement journey of any kind and are fully aware and take responsibility for your own results holding Peggy McColl and Dynamic Destinies Inc. harmless.

This is intended for informational purposes only and should not be used as the primary basis for an investment decision. Consult a financial advisor for your personal situation. Please consider the investment objectives, risks, fees, and expenses carefully before investing in anything. Past performance does not guarantee future results.

For more disclaimers that may apply, please view the most up to date information on:

http://www.peggymccoll.com

Cover design by Killer Covers
Book layout by Trace Haskins
Editing by Kathryn Young
First Edition, 2022

Dedication

My brother, Gary McColl
August 20, 1950 – June 18, 2000

My friend and mentor, Bob Proctor
July 5, 1934 – February 3, 2022

.

Praise for Savy Wisdom 2: The Sequel

"If you loved Savy Wisdom you'll love the sequel just as much, if not more! This book offers the reader an authentic and vulnerable window into Sophie's life trajectory, and how her strength of character, and positive mindset, helped her overcome heartbreak and serious health challenges. Sophie's victory doesn't happen by chance, she makes it happen. Don't pass this book by; it is inspirational and will leave you with valuable gems of advice."

~ L.L. Tremblay, Author of Seven Roses

"McColl is one of those gifted authors who writes page-turning plots about complex characters you root for while simultaneously imbuing life lessons in the process. Savy Wisdom 2 is a must read."

~ M. Shawn Petersen,
Author of Stella And The Timekeepers

"Wow comes to my mind! I read Savy Wisdom four times, but Savy Wisdom 2: The Sequel is going to 'blow your mind'. It is a true page turner; I could not put it down. Peggy continues to share such valuable lessons in personal growth life. There is not a person in the world that does not relate to at least one story. Savy Wisdom continues to inspire and positively influence hundreds of millions of souls worldwide with Peggy's wisdom, light, insights, guidance, and awareness. Savy Wisdom 2: The Sequel is full of love, tears, tension, excitement, sadness, surprises, and it keeps you on tip toes until you reach the end. Life is a phenomenal journey and if you choose it to be, it can be the best adventure and celebration you ever experience. The lessons learned throughout both Savy Wisdom books are priceless and leave every heart with believing that 'I AM POSSIBLE'. I simply love, love, looooove it!"

~ Vladimira Kuna, International Bestseller of The Bible of The Masterminds

"Inspirational, educational and wisdom from the best... Did I mention emotional? That too! Get this book ... your future self will thank you."

~ Anders Hansen, Illusionist,
Key-Note Performer and Change-Maker

"Savy Wisdom has delivered yet again, but this time with even bigger and more powerful life changing lessons. Whatever challenge you may have happening now, this book will be a guiding light in your life. Thank you, Peggy, you are truly an inspiration."

~ Roderick Telfer, Entrepreneur

"Savy Wisdom 2 picks us up where the first book left off and carries us through the next chapter of Sophie's life in a fast-paced emotional roller-coaster of challenges and big wins, intertwined with valuable advice. The wealth of impactful life lessons in this book made me take notice of how I can apply these lessons to effectively improve my own life. I've already incorporated *The Easy Code* into my life script – and if you don't know what that means, you'll have to read Savy Wisdom 2 to find out!"

~ Jenny Gough, Author and Entrepreneur

"I read the sequel to Savy Wisdom in one sitting... I couldn't put it down! Sophie has grown so much since the first book, and you too will be captivated by her story. Loved it! Congrats Peggy on another successful book."

~ Jayne Lowell,
Co-Founder S&J Training Solutions

"Savy Wisdom 2: The Sequel is packed with story after story that demonstrate how we always have a choice in the way we create our destiny, even under extreme conditions where life seems out of our hands. I read the entire book in one sitting, yet the lessons are eternal. Enjoy it, and takes notes – which will help you integrate Savy Wisdom in your own life."

~ Trace Haskins
Author of Prosperous On Purpose

Table of Contents

Chapter 1

Life could not be more beautiful. My heart has been filled with love and gratitude ever since Savy came into my life. Every now and then, I return to the neighborhood park near my parent's house, where I met him for the first time. It remains my most memorable, life-changing moment to date.

Back then, my soul felt trapped inside a sad and disenchanted body, and all I could think about was how to end my life. Spirit must have heard my cry for help that day and sent a messenger to my rescue. Savy's words of wisdom saved my life. From that day forward, I escaped the weight of negativity. I became the self-assured, positive, and fearless person that had been hiding inside me for so long.

Larger than life is how I feel now. I am capable and able to attract all that I want and desire for myself and for my family. Everything in and around my life now feels so abundant. Some days I wonder if my heart is big enough to host this much richness, but it is. I know that now.

On the day my first book was released, it happened to be a beautiful evening with a clear sky. Dusk was approaching, and the sky had a picturesque orange glow. I finished dressing and jumped in my car to head downtown to the Crown Hotel for my book launch party. I had been wondering what a book launch party would be like. I had never been to one before.

I pulled into the parking garage. I intended to find a parking spot close to the elevators. I didn't want to walk too far as I had new high-heel shoes on. I drove around the garage from floor to floor looking, and there simply weren't any available spots anywhere.

I decided to wait for someone to leave. I pulled my car to the side, let it idle, and waited. No one left, and more cars were arriving looking for a parking spot as well.

For the few minutes I waited, I found myself lost in worried thoughts about my husband, Eddie. Eddie was scheduled to go with me to the party, but he called that afternoon to say he was working late and would meet me at the hotel. Eddie's behavior had changed since I received the advance for my book. He seemed withdrawn and somewhat unavailable. He would often work late and not make it home on time for dinner.

I began to wonder if Eddie was jealous of my success. To me, it didn't make sense that he could be envious of something that provided me with a seven-figure advance, which benefited both of us. The funds allowed us to pay cash for our home and to put money into investments. Financially, we were in a very healthy position. Something was bothering him, and I decided I would make it my mission to find out what it was.

It was obviously a busy night at the hotel. The parking garage was a large, multi-level building that probably held hundreds of vehicles.

It was thirty minutes until my book launch event, and I began feeling a little anxious. I certainly didn't want to be late for my own party. Ten more minutes passed as I sat and waited for someone to leave the garage.

An idea came to mind. The hotel had to have a valet service. Quickly, I put my car in gear and headed toward the hotel's entrance. Fortunately, I was right. Valet service was available, and I pulled in. I hopped out of my car, handed the keys to the young man, and gave him a tip.

My first book, *Destiny Treasure*, was launching that day. My publisher and I had been planning and preparing for the launch for months. *Destiny Treasure* is a romantic novel blended with tragedy. The book has creative twists and turns that leave the reader on the edge of their seat right up until the very end. As much as the editor and the advanced readers loved the book, I was wondering how the rest of the world would feel about it. Would the readers love it? Would people criticize it? Would it have that word-of-mouth appeal that I had heard about? Answers to these questions will be revealed in due time.

My publisher, Terragon Publishing, was an absolute pleasure to deal with throughout the entire publishing process. We had many meetings at their headquarters, and they were always fun and enjoyable. I am sure it helped that Savy, the owner of the publishing house, was my friend. I was pleased with my treatment by the staff. The employees seemed to have a mandate to make every person who entered their office building feel important. I suspected that was a recommendation from the owner himself.

Terragon had their own in-house media team that scheduled multiple radio and television interviews, along with bookstore signings for me to promote my book. They hired the best media trainer in the business, and he worked with me for several days, ensuring that I was media-ready and my answers were succinct yet effective. There were billboard ads placed, and magazine and newspaper ads too.

Savy had asked me what I would love as far as the results of my book being launched, and I had my answer ready.

"There is only one outcome for *Destiny Treasure*, and that is a mega-hit success! This book is going straight to the top of the most prestigious best-seller list, and it is going to stay there for years. I see this book translated into more than forty languages and sold all over the world."

"Terrific. I see that for you, Sophie. Here's what I suggest that you do. Write out an affirmation or goal statement that reflects the outcome you desire. Repeat it every day. Most important, as you know for goal achievement, is to *feel* as if it is already done. Every day give thanks for your success. See the bestseller list in your mind and see your book on top. The clearer the image, the better it will feel."

Prior to the launch, I created mocked-up images reflecting my book as a best-seller and placed them on my vision board. I believed millions of copies of my book would be sold within the first year. It was a lofty goal, but I understood that my responsibility was to feel as if it was already done and to promote it like crazy.

As I walked into the hotel lobby, I smiled when I saw signage with my book cover on it and arrows pointing toward a hallway. *Follow the yellow brick road* came to mind. I will follow the arrows and see where they lead me.

As I walked down the hallway to where the hotel's ballroom was located, I noticed a large crowd of people. There were large vertical banners with my book cover, a large WELCOME sign, and a sign for REGISTRATION. Servers lingered around offering hors d'oeuvres and champagne. It appeared the guests were being held outside the ballroom until it was time to open the doors.

Oh my goodness! I thought. I stopped in my tracks and realized this was all for *me* and for my book! There were people everywhere. The packed parking lot now made sense. I took a quick look around for Eddie. I couldn't wait to share this with him.

My literary agent, Colleen, spotted me in the crowd and raced over to greet me.

"Geez, Sophie, I was starting to wonder if you were coming," Colleen said in a joking manner. "Get stuck in traffic or something?"

"Sorry. It took me a while to get my car parked. Great to see you. Is Savy here? I'd love to see him."

"Yes, he's in the green room. Follow me, and I'll take you to him."

As Colleen led me into the ballroom, I stopped for a moment. The room was decorated spectacularly with gold streamers, balloons, enormous flower arrangements, banners, and a large stage with a couple of giant screens, one on the left side of the stage and the other on the right. Each screen had an image of my book. It was larger than life. There was a long, raised table at the back of the room for audio and video, and several gentlemen sat there appearing to be busy. There had to be a thousand chairs set up in the room, maybe more.

Colleen took me to the green room where Savy was sitting with the managing editor of the publishing house, Benjamin Savoie. He was a kind, soft-spoken and handsome man. I reflected on the day I had met Benjamin. He walked into the boardroom while I was meeting with the publicity team, and he made an instant and positive first impression.

Savy stood and gave me a big hug. "Ready for a great night? This is all to celebrate you and your book, *Destiny Treasure.*"

"Oh my, you have outdone yourself. I have never been to a book launch party and was not expecting this. I am blown away. This is extraordinary, and I'm filled with gratitude. Thank you, Savy."

"You look amazing. Where's Eddie?" Savy asked.

I appreciated the compliment. That day I had gone to the salon and had my hair and nails done. I wanted to look my best. I bought a beautiful new designer suit and new shoes. Savy once told me, "You have one chance to make a first impression, so make it a great one."

Before I could answer Savy's question about Eddie, one of the sound engineers entered the green room to let us know it was time to take our seats. The show was about to begin.

"The show?" I asked inquiringly. "What show?"

With that, Savy and I were whisked into the ballroom and directed to sit in the front row. I saved a seat next to me for Eddie. Loud, energetic, upbeat music started. The ballroom doors burst open, and hundreds of people poured in and raced for a seat.

As the guests settled, the lights dimmed, and the stage came to life. Music began, and a singer walked onto the stage. He began singing "The Music of the Night," a song from my favorite musical, *The Phantom of the Opera*. Ballet dancers graced the stage in beautiful costumes. It was breathtaking, and the audience erupted into a standing ovation when they finished their performance.

Savy then walked onto the stage to speak next. I had never seen him speak in front of a live audience before. He captured the audience by his mere presence. Talk about spellbinding. The way he moved on the stage, from side to side, connecting with the audience. He held them in the palm of his hand and used his voice volume, inflection, and tonality to make each point so perfectly. I had already learned so much from this man, and I could see I still had a lot to learn.

This was truly a night to remember. The performances were all top notch and first class, from the opening act to the comedian and the hypnotist. All the entertainers magically tied in the book title or messages from the book—that blew my mind.

As the show was about to wrap up, Savy went back on stage and invited me to join him. I was wondering if I was going to have to speak. I hadn't been given any notice, nor was I asked to prepare anything, but I discovered that Savy felt it fitting that I say a few words.

I joined him on the stage and looked over the smiling crowd. I thanked everyone for attending, shared my gratitude for my family, the hotel staff, and the people who put the event together: the entertainers, my publisher, and of course, Savy. I spoke for a few minutes and let everyone know how I met Savy. I heard a few gasps in the audience when I said that I had gone to the park that day to end my life, and this wonderful man had saved me. I told them that dreams could come true. You must believe it!

People were then directed to a side table where they could purchase a signed, autographed copy of *Destiny Treasure*. I had autographed books days earlier when I was at the publishing house, which made it easy for me to talk and mingle with the guests.

When I had been on stage, with a clear view of the room, I had looked for Eddie. Every chair in the ballroom was filled. I saw some familiar faces, and my entire family was there: my mom, dad, sister, brother, sister-in-law, and nieces and nephews; but still, I couldn't see Eddie anywhere. His parents and siblings weren't there either. How could Eddie have missed this? He knew how important this was to me. I suddenly hoped that he was okay and hadn't gotten into an accident. I felt a pull of emotions from upset to concern.

Chapter 2

On the drive home, I reflected on the spectacular launch party. I was smiling from ear to ear. I felt so good. The evening was truly special. The only downside was Eddie not showing up. I tried his cell phone, but it just rolled to voicemail.

When I got to our house and entered the garage, I saw Eddie's car parked in the usual spot. I knew then that he hadn't been in an accident, so perhaps he was ill, and that was the reason he didn't make it to the event.

I walked into the house and found Eddie already in bed sleeping. I was dumbfounded. No note, no call, no explanation. What in the world is going on?

Eddie and I married a couple of years before the launch of my book. Within a relatively short time, I had received an offer to publish my first book and received an astonishing advance of $2,400,000. I couldn't have been happier, and I thought Eddie was happy too. He seemed happy in the beginning.

After I received the funds from the publisher, Eddie began to withdraw. He became distant. He worked long hours and was rarely home for dinner. I made some effort to ask him if something was bothering him, but he shrugged it off and said that his work was just overwhelming right now. Being an independent woman and having a lot on my plate, I didn't mind the time to myself, but I knew we weren't functioning the way I felt a married couple should.

I still suspected his moodiness had something to do with money. In my mind, my money was our money. My success was our success, but apparently, Eddie didn't seem to feel the same way. He told me once that he felt that he should be the provider for the household and felt uncomfortable that it was my money that paid for most things. In that way, he said he felt inadequate. I did my best to reassure him, but I knew that it wasn't up to me to cause him to feel better about himself. He had to do that himself.

I never got an answer as to why Eddie skipped the launch party. He said something the next morning about not feeling well and just needing to catch up on his sleep. I told myself to be patient and to let him work it out.

Meanwhile, the efforts to promote my book, *Destiny Treasure*, were working like magic. The book earned its way onto the bestseller list during the first week of the launch. This was one milestone reached. We were off to a great start; however, I knew that it was essential to keep promoting the book to accomplish my bigger goal.

The publisher had arranged for several national media appearances and bookstore signings, which invited a lot of travel for me. I loved to travel. They offered to include Eddie on my trips and pay for his travel, but he declined. I would often call him from the road, but I mostly got his voicemail, and when we did connect, the calls were short.

There was a stretch of time when I had been away for two straight weeks. I was starting to feel homesick. I wanted to be home, sleeping in our bed, and waking up with my husband. I managed to move some things around, and this gave me the opportunity to go home a couple of days earlier than planned. Instead of telling Eddie I was coming home, I decided to surprise him. I thought he would be happy to have me back earlier than planned. I made a reservation at a restaurant I knew he liked, and I resolved to work on the barriers that had come up in my marriage. We might even need to get some counseling to help with our communication.

The flight home was smooth and on time. I grabbed a taxi from the airport and headed home. It was early evening. When I arrived home, I noticed lights were on in the house and assumed Eddie was home from work. I walked in but didn't immediately see him. The kitchen was unusually messy. There were two empty wine glasses on the kitchen counter, and one of them had lipstick on it. This surprised me. Maybe Eddie's mom had come over for a visit. I knew she loved her wine.

As I walked toward the master suite, I could hear laughter coming from the bedroom. Suddenly, my stomach flipped. I was shaking as I grabbed the handle to the door. When I walked into the bedroom, I found my husband Eddie in bed with a woman who worked at Eddie's company. Her name was Mallory, and I had met her a couple of times. It shocked me. My mouth was gaped open. Words wouldn't come out. I didn't know what to do. I felt as if I was going to be sick to my stomach.

The first words out of my mouth were loud and directed at Mallory. "Get out! Get out of my bed and my home! Who the hell do you think you are?"

I was so upset and had to go to the washroom to vomit. I couldn't believe this was happening. I felt out of control of my emotions. As Mallory hurriedly dressed, I confronted Eddie and screamed some more.

"You too . . . get out! Take your shit and get the hell out of here. We're done!" I had zero tolerance for cheating, and Eddie knew it. He wanted to talk.

"Now you want to talk? I have tried for the last two years to talk with you. To find out what was bothering you. Instead, you betray me? How long has this been going on? Never mind, it doesn't matter. We are done. Our marriage is over. I am not interested in talking with you anymore. I want you out of here tonight. Gather your stuff and go," I demanded.

Eddie knew enough to know I was serious. I realized there wasn't any other vehicle in the driveway, so Mallory must have come home with Eddie. She left the house first. Eddie followed.

Once he was gone, I sat on the sofa and cried my heart out. I couldn't believe this was happening. I realized my marriage was over. There was no going back. To me, adultery was the ultimate betrayal.

My grief quickly turned to anger. I got off the sofa and walked into the walk-in closet adjacent to the master and started to tear Eddie's clothes off the hangers and threw them on the floor. I grabbed large garbage bags and threw his clothes and all his belongings into half a dozen bags. I wasn't carefully folding his clothes. I dragged all six bags to the garage.

I took the framed wedding photo that was beside our bed and tossed it in the garbage. I pulled the sheets off the bed, along with the comforter, throw pillows, sleeping pillows, and threw it all in the garbage. I could have easily put them in the washing machine, but the thought of sleeping in that bedding again made me feel ill. I would simply buy new bedding. Maybe a new bed too.

Once I finished discarding Eddie's personal belongings, I couldn't sleep, and I certainly wasn't going to go to bed in the master bedroom. All night long, I went from sadness to disbelief and back to anger. I laid on the sofa and didn't sleep at all.

When morning arrived, I called my lawyer. I requested that he draft up a separation agreement immediately. It may have seemed fast, but I was an action-driven person, and as far as I was concerned, the sooner I took care of getting the wheels for divorce in motion, the better.

Eddie tried to call me several times. At first, I refused to answer the phone. I had nothing to say, and I didn't want to hear his voice. I wasn't really a black or white person, except when it came to cheating. Early in our relationship, I told Eddie that I would work through any challenge we had, but cheating would end the relationship.

I knew I had to talk with Eddie at some point, and he would need to come and get his stuff. The next time he called, I answered the phone. Calmly I told Eddie that his belongings would be in the garage, and he could use the garage code to enter, but I had already ordered a locksmith to change the locks on the house, and the locks would be changed that day. I also told him that I called a lawyer, and the divorce papers were being drawn up.

Eddie knew I meant business. He wasn't arguing or trying to convince me to take him back. He apologized profusely for hurting me. He told me that he wouldn't dispute the divorce agreement, and anything I wanted, he would agree to. I believe his guilt was directing his response. He told me that the house and the money we put in investments was mine. He didn't want anything. He felt that it wasn't his anyway. In a way, I was happy about that. Legally he was entitled to half of everything, but I wasn't going to argue if he didn't want anything.

For the first few days following the discovery of Eddie and Mallory, anger was my dominant emotion. In one way, it was my survival mechanism, but I knew it wasn't healthy. I would have to forgive him, but I certainly wasn't going to forget. Forgiveness didn't mean I was taking him back, but for me to move on, it was necessary.

Divorce felt like a failure to me. I felt like a failure. Once again, I reflected back to the day I met Savy. I went to the park that day, determined to end my life because my high school sweetheart had ended our relationship.

I remember feeling so distraught that I had no will to live, which was a culmination of many years of feeling unlovable. This time it was different. I knew I was lovable and decided to be open and honest with myself and figure out the lessons in this experience.

As much as getting a divorce was a painful experience, I knew there had to be a great lesson in it. I started to ask myself questions: What role did I play in attracting this into my life? I wanted to be completely honest with myself. This awareness would allow me to not repeat these mistakes in the future. More empowering questions came to mind: What is great about this? How will I use this experience in a positive way?

I knew life would go on. I understood the importance of managing my emotions and choosing to stay away from destructive emotions. Anger was toxic and would only bring me harm. Any time I felt anger, I would switch to forgiveness and let the anger go.

It was time for a new chapter in my life. I knew I was in the driver's seat and could set the direction and destination. Going through a divorce at such a young age ended up being my most painful life experience but brought about my greatest learning about who I was and what I wanted.

Chapter 3

Three months had passed since Eddie moved out. I was adjusting to single life and finding it easy to fill my time. I was grateful the divorce was in motion. Creating the divorce papers was easy because Eddie agreed to everything. He didn't even bother getting a lawyer. He said it wasn't necessary. He believed we could work out our own arrangement. We opened a file at the court and scheduled a date to stand before the judge.

As I approached the courtroom, Eddie was walking toward me from the other direction. I wasn't sure if I should say anything or not but decided to face the situation and be polite. I paused and waited for Eddie.

"Hi Eddie, how are you doing?" I asked, not knowing how or if he was going to respond.

I had wondered how I was going to feel, knowing I would see him. Surprisingly, I felt nothing. I had no feelings of being upset whatsoever. I was grateful for the ability to focus my attention on thoughts that made me feel good. I had already moved on from what happened with Eddie and only reflected on the good memories of the early days of our marriage.

"Hi Sophie," he responded with a small smile. "I'm doing okay. Thank you for asking. How about you?"

"Doing great, thank you."

Pleasantly surprised by the warmth of his tone, I opened the courtroom door, and we walked in and took a seat together.

The judge called our names and asked us to stand. He asked if we both agreed to the conditions of this divorce. We both responded with an affirmative reply at the exact same time. He confirmed that we do not have any children, and we both responded affirmatively. I suspected the judge didn't have many divorce cases this clear cut. The judge said something like "granted," but I couldn't hear him well. He stamped the document that was in front of him and told us, "That will be all. Your divorce is granted." With that, we both stood and left the courtroom.

Eddie paused and glanced my way. "Have a nice day, Sophie," he said sincerely.

"You too, Eddie," I responded with a nod.

As I walked away, I felt a great sense of relief. Eddie had a right to half of everything I had, including our magnificent dream house, but he wanted none of it. I hadn't been sure whether he would change his mind, but he didn't. I thought perhaps I should be celebrating or something, but in my heart, this didn't feel like a thing to celebrate. We were told that within thirty days, the divorce would be final.

My new life moved on. My business was growing in leaps and bounds, and I worked twelve to sixteen hours a day. The success of my book brought me a lot of attention, and requests came in by the droves from people asking me to guide them on how to write a book and make it a best seller. I realized I could effectively help new and existing authors by creating a program, and so I did just that.

The weekdays were filled with work, but the weekends were reserved for me time. Inevitably, on many Friday afternoons, my phone would ring and either my brother or my sister-in-law called asking if the kids could come for a visit.

"Of course, they are always welcome here," became my standard response.

My nieces and nephews loved coming to Aunt Sophie's for sleepovers on the weekend. We always had a ton of fun. They thought I was the cool aunt. They loved my home, especially the games room, theater room, and backyard. After a weekend with them, I would be exhausted, but it was a wonderful kind of exhaustion.

Mostly, they loved my resort-style backyard with the pool, hot tub, and outdoor summerhouse. After moving into the home, I hired a company to build the pool and hot tub along with an outdoor gazebo with a bar, fireplace, change room, and sitting area. It was built with remote-controlled pulldown enclosers. On the cooler evenings, the enclosers could be brought down. When the fireplace was lit, it was rather cozy in there. The sitting area had a large sectional sofa, and since there was a large screen television on the wall above the fireplace, we would often go out to the summerhouse and watch a movie. Sometimes we fell asleep on the large sectional and woke up in the morning. The kids thought this was the best. Their joy brought me joy.

On one weekend, I made different plans. Savy had called and invited me to his home for dinner. This was a first. I was pleased to get the invitation and graciously accepted. I asked him, "What can I bring?" and he responded with "your smiling face."

I was excited to get the chance to meet Savy's wife, Carol. They had been married over fifty years, and, according to him, they were more in love today than they had ever been.

"I'm looking forward to meeting Carol," I said. "It's wonderful to know a couple so deeply in love after more than fifty years of marriage. I wouldn't know what that's like. My marriage barely lasted a couple of years."

I believe Savy felt the tone of my disappointment, and he responded. "Don't mistake the longevity of a marriage as a success. Many couples who have been married for decades are unhappy. Unlike my marriage, most of our friends are miserable together. They stay together because of their kids, and even after their children move out on their own, they stay out of habit. Staying together doesn't mean you're in a successful marriage. Give thanks that you discovered early in the relationship, before you started a family, that Eddie was not the type of man you want to invest the rest of your life with. I know how important commitment is to you,

Sophie, and I believe, one day, you'll find the perfect soulmate."

The idea of another relationship hadn't been on my mind at that time. I was open to it; I was simply not focusing on it. Instead, I completely submerged myself in my work. I was happy. Truly happy.

It was Saturday and time to head over to Savy and Carol's home for dinner. He said they eat early and asked that I arrive between 4:30 and 5:00 pm. At 4:45 pm, I drove up to their gate.

Savy and Carol lived in a castle-like home on a lake. It was a spectacular home. To get into the property, you had to be buzzed in. I pushed the buzzer, the gates opened wide, and I drove in.

There was one other car in the driveway when I arrived. It was a beautiful new Mercedes convertible. *Hot car,* I thought. I wondered if Savy or Carol drove it. I got out of my car and stood on the driveway, looking around. This place was massive, and the landscaping was out of this world. Every bush was trimmed impeccably. The lawn looked like a soft, even, flowing green blanket.

The front door opened as I approached the front steps. Savy was there to greet me.

"Welcome, Sophie. It is a pleasure to have you in our home."

"Thank you so much for the invitation. You have a beautiful setting here. You're relatively close to the city, but it feels so private," I remarked as I handed him a large bouquet of flowers that I brought for Carol.

"It helps when you are on a five-acre property," Savy teased. "Thank you for the beautiful flowers."

As I walked into the entrance of the home, I gasped. I had seen homes like this in magazines or in movies but had never stepped inside such a magnificent structure. The ceiling had to be forty feet high in the entranceway. You could see the upstairs from the foyer, and the circular staircase was exceptional. The décor was divine. "Wow," was the only word that came out of my mouth.

"Follow me. I would like to show you my favorite room in the house." Savy asked me to follow him to his library. The library was at the end of the hallway, tucked away in its own little wing. The library had high ceilings with a ladder that rolled along rows and rows of books. The room had a wood-burning fireplace, a fire was burning, and it smelled divine. I loved the sound of the crackling of the wood. This room had a magnificent warmth about it, and I felt like grabbing one of the books from the floor-to-ceiling bookshelf and curling up in the comfy loveseat and getting lost in a story.

Savy was proud of his library. He said, "A home without books is like a house without windows." He loved to read biographies. There must have been hundreds and hundreds of books in his library.

As Savy and I stood there talking about some of his favorite biographies, I felt the presence of another person enter the room. I turned to find Benjamin Savoie standing in the doorway.

"Sophie, I hope you don't mind, but I invited Benjamin to join us tonight. You remember Benjamin?" Savy said with a sheepish smile on his face.

What is he up to? Is this a setup? Was he playing matchmaker?

"Yes, of course, I remember Benjamin. Nice to see you again." I stretched out my hand to shake his.

"Please call me Benny. All my closest friends do. Nice to see you too."

Instantly I had a flashback to the day I met Benjamin, aka Benny, at the Terragon Publishing headquarters. I had an unusual head-to-toe goosebump experience the day I met him, and I had no earthly idea why. I remember looking at him with a strange feeling of attraction. I also remember dismissing the feeling as I was married at the time.

The evening was an evening to remember. Carol was lovelier than Savy had described her. She had a wicked sense of humor and told stories and had us all laughing until our cheeks ached. They arranged for caterers to prepare and present the meal, which made it easier to converse with everyone. I felt as if we were eating in one of the finest five-star restaurants. The food was exquisite and mouth-watering, but the company was the best. Benny was easygoing and quite worldly. I could tell he was an intelligent man, and he sure was easy on the eyes.

It was getting late, and I could see from Savy's face that he was tired. He was an early-to-bed, early-to-rise kind of person, so I felt it was time to head out. As I decided to leave, Benny said it was time for him to leave as well.

Benny and I said our goodbyes to Savy and Carol and found ourselves standing in the driveway. As we both stood there, there was a bit of awkward silence, and neither one of us moved. I could tell he wanted to say something. He broke the silence. "Sophie, would you like to go and grab a coffee at The Morning Owl?"

The Morning Owl was a local coffee shop. Many of the people at the publishing house frequented this place.

"Is it open now?" I asked. "I am fairly certain it closes after lunchtime. I don't believe it's open in the evening. You're welcome to come to my place. I have coffee."

As soon as the words left my lips, I felt trepidation. What in the world was I doing? I'm inviting a man to my home—and it's late—and I hardly know him!

Since my divorce, I hadn't dated anyone. I had received invitations for dates but turned them down. In this case, I felt that I could trust Benny. After all, Savy trusted him. I don't think Savy would invite anyone to his home that he didn't know, like, and trust, so I convinced myself it was going to be perfectly fine.

Benny followed me home. He was the owner of that hot little convertible Mercedes that was parked in Savy's driveway. He had great taste in vehicles. I found it interesting that we both drove a Mercedes. He dressed impeccably and exuded confidence. I found him to be very sexy too, and I was fascinated by my attraction to him.

Once we arrived at my house, we chose to have a glass of wine out in the summerhouse by the pool rather than a cup of coffee. I rarely drank coffee at night, so I was happy when Benny accepted my offer of a glass of vino. Before long, the bottle of wine was empty, and we were chatting up a storm and having lots of laughs.

Benny knew I was divorced but had no idea what had happened. I could tell he was being respectful, but I also sensed that he wanted to find out more about my marriage breakup.

After another glass of wine was in me, I was an open book. Ask me anything, and I'll tell you everything seemed to be what happened when I drank any amount of alcohol. I wasn't much of a drinker, as I rarely drank, but when I did, it usually hit me quickly. After two glasses of wine, I was feeling a little tipsy. Good thing I wasn't driving. Then I realized that Benny had driven his car to my place. He can't drive until he is sober or until the morning. I had plenty of guest rooms, and when the conversation runs out, I'll offer for him to stay and avoid driving under the influence.

After I shared the story of Eddie's infidelity, Benny asked me if I was feeling any anger. He said, "Aren't you upset at what he did to you? You seem calm and accepting. You didn't deserve to be treated like that."

I appreciated Benny's kind words and compassion.

"I've moved on. I wish him well and only send him loving thoughts. It is what it is. I've forgiven him, moved past, and harvested the good. I will never forget what Savy told me when he said, *If you're going to slander someone, write it in the sand, by the water's edge.*"

Benny and I talked and talked until the sun came up the next morning. It was hard to believe, for either one of us, that it was morning already. We laughed that it was time for that cup of coffee after all, and I made some in a French press.

As Benny stood up to leave, he turned to me and asked, "Would you be available for dinner tomorrow night? I'd love to take you to this little quaint Italian restaurant that I discovered. The food is out of this world. You like Italian, don't you?"

"Italian is my absolute fav. Yes, I'd love to. Thank you. What time should I be ready?"

"How's six for you? I'll be here to pick you up. Dress comfortably so we can go for a stroll along the canal after dinner."

As Benny drove away, I watched him from the window. I felt such a warmth come over me. It was the strangest feeling. This guy must have put a spell on me. I was convinced.

Chapter 4

After catching up on a night of missed sleep, I felt eager about the upcoming date with Benny. *Is it too soon to be dating?* I wondered. Something inside me felt that a relationship with Benny could be something magnificent. I decided to see how things would unfold.

Benny arrived promptly at 5:55 pm to pick me up for our dinner date. He may have noticed my smile and nod of appreciation for his early arrival.

Without me asking him a thing, he began, "Many years ago, when I played competitive hockey, my coach told every player on the team to arrive five to fifteen minutes before the practice time started. He said if you arrive on time, you're late. He drilled it into our heads to be early, and it served me in sports, and it serves me now in business."

The restaurant was called Angelina's. After we were seated at the table, Benny wasted no time and started asking questions. The night before, we had talked mostly about light-hearted topics and laughed a lot. This time, he asked many important and serious questions, and when I finished answering one question, he was on to another. "What is most important to you? What drives you? Where do you see yourself in five years? What inspires you to write books? Why did you start your own business?"

I felt like this was an inquisition, though a pleasant one. Maybe he simply wanted to get to know everything about me. I was equally interested in him, and with every firing of a question my way, I shot one back his way. It appeared to be a question-and-answer tennis match.

By the end of the meal, we had a great understanding of who we are, what our values are, and what is most important in our lives. Our compatibility became very evident within a short period of time. There was an undeniable attraction between the two of us as well.

After dinner, we took a long stroll along the canal. Benny reached out to hold my hand. He had large, masculine hands, yet they were soft to the touch. I felt safe with him. I could feel the coolness of the night air and shivered a little. Benny took his jacket off and draped it over my shoulders. He was a true gentleman.

One date turned to a second one. Pretty soon, we were together every day. My weekends with my nieces and nephews became weekends with Benny too. He fit right in. The kids loved him. He was playful and fun. He made the kids laugh and would play with them for hours. The stamina he had was extraordinary.

Months passed, and we were a dynamic pair having the time of our lives. I made room for Benny's belongings in my closet. He started to have more and more clothes at my home. One evening, I made a comment about that.

"Benny, you're here now every single evening. Please don't get me wrong, this is not a complaint, as a matter of fact, I love it. The reason why I mention it is because your house sits empty. What about entertaining the idea of renting out your house and moving in here? Is that something you might be open to? You are here all the time anyway." As the words escaped my lips, I felt my tummy do a little summersault. I wasn't sure if I was feeling fear or excitement.

Benny looked at me with a surprised look on his face. For a moment, he didn't say anything. I assumed he was trying to figure out how to let me down gently.

His answer confirmed my assumption was incorrect. "I'd love that. Are you sure this is what you want?" he responded. "This is a great idea as I could easily rent out my house."

"I wouldn't have asked if I didn't mean it. Yes, of course, I am sure. I have never felt surer of anything in my life."

Spring came early that year. Blossoms were on the trees, the fresh smell of nature was in the air, and the birds were singing. I decided to do something I hadn't done for quite some time and requested to meet Savy in the park. I called him and asked him if he wanted to meet. He gratefully accepted and agreed to meet me the following morning at 6:30 am.

After a quick stop at The Morning Owl, I arrived with a couple of cappuccinos in hand, and I sat down on the special park bench with ten minutes to spare. As usual, Savy arrived a few minutes early too.

We exchanged our usual pleasantries, talked about the weather, drank our cappuccinos, and then got right down to the reason for the meeting.

"What's on your mind, Sophie?" Savy asked.

"Well, I am having a bit of a challenge with keeping my thinking straight when it comes to relationships. As you know, Benny and I moved in together—"

Savy interrupted. "Hang on a second, please. What did you say? Are you and Benjamin Savoie living together?"

Before I could answer, questions raced around my mind. Was this not acceptable to Savy? Was he upset? Did he think we moved too quickly?

As I had these thoughts, Savy continued.

"If so, I am delighted! You two make a perfect couple. I invited the two of you to dinner several months ago on purpose. I strongly felt that you would make a great couple. I could see how you are different in some ways yet complement each other in other ways. This is wonderful news. Truly."

"Thank you so much. I appreciate that. I had a feeling that dinner was a setup, and that reminds me, thank you for the setup." I smiled as I spoke.

"Wait, you said you were having a challenge. What kind of challenge are you having, and how can I help?" Savy asked.

"My challenge is believing the relationship is going to last. I've only had two other serious relationships in my life, as you know, and they both ended. I loved both Chad and Eddie when we were together, but with Benny, it is so different. I am so deeply in love with him that I almost feel panicky. I feel fear. I'm afraid I'm going to do something to sabotage the relationship, or I fear he will end it. Sometimes I get so consumed by these thoughts that I become insecure. I don't want to think like that. What do I do to change it?"

Savy always had the perfect answer for everything. He reached out and put his hand on mine.

"Oh, my dear Sophie. What would you love? Remember that powerful four-word question I asked of you before? Ask yourself that question now as it relates to your relationship with Benny. What would you love for your relationship? Once you determine that—and I am sure you already know—then decide what you need to *believe* to have that outcome. You must feel as if you already have the type of relationship you desire. This is really a three-step process. Here are the three steps."

I interrupted Savy before he could go on.

"Wait, wait, I want to write this down!"

"You don't need to write this down as I am certain you'll remember it. It is an easy solution for anything you want to manifest, but if you want to write it down, I'll wait while you pull out your journal and pen. Plus, I have gone over this with you before. You will recognize these steps."

"Okay, I'm ready."

Savy continued. "Step One. Answer this question: *What would you love?*

Step Two. *Determine what you need to believe to have that.*

Step Three. *Feel as if you already have it in your life.*"

I nodded as I wrote them down. "Yes, I do recognize these steps."

"Allow me to expand. The reason why you are feeling trepidation or discomfort with your present relationship is because you are allowing your previous experience to determine how this one is going to go. Your past does not have to determine your future. Give your attention only to the outcomes you desire. The second part of this exercise is to determine the beliefs that are necessary to create your desired outcome. Let's walk through this together right now. Tell me, Sophie. What would you love?"

I had written down every word he said. Answering the question would be easy.

"I would love a fun, loyal, committed, honest, romantic, connected, enjoyable, loving relationship with my soulmate." The words rolled off my tongue with ease.

"Terrific. What do you need to *believe* to have that?" Savy asked.

"Hmnnn . . . okay . . . well, I suppose I need to believe I am worthy of it. I need to believe that I am also a fun, loyal, committed, honest, romantic, loving person. I need to believe we are together forever, and our relationship gets better and better every day in every way." I could feel myself growing stronger as I connected to this answer.

"Alright! That was easy. However, you must believe it in your heart. My next question for you is, now that you have that, how do you feel?"

"Amazing!" I shouted. "I feel so good, so relaxed, so grateful, so happy."

"Outstanding. Here's what you must do. Every single day, affirm to yourself that you are already enjoying the type of relationship you desire. Only give energy to the desired outcome. Feel it in your heart. If you find yourself getting off track, perhaps feeling that fear rise, switch it. *Focus* on those three steps, and you will be right back on track. If you need to switch from fear to faith many times an hour, do it. It won't be long until the dominant thoughts and feelings are only directed on the outcomes you want. You will find your old way of thinking fade away."

Feeling uplifted, I knew I had the perfect answer to my challenge. I wondered how it was that Savy always knew what to say.

"You are always so giving to me. Is there anything I can do for you, Mr. Vaughan?"

"Are we getting formal now, Miss Edwards?"

As Savy said my last name, I briefly wondered if I should change my name back to my maiden name, Collins. My business was built around the name Sophie Edwards. My book, already a huge success and bestseller, carried that name.

Savy picked up his hat and stood to leave.

"Simply follow through with my recommendations is all I ask. I care about you. I love seeing you happy, and, right now, you are the happiest I have ever seen you."

Before I left the park that day, there was one other thing on my mind that I quickly mentioned to Savy. Two weeks prior, I had discovered a lump on my neck. It was approximately the size of a grape. I had also mentioned it to Benny and told him I was going to get it checked out. It was in my neck, near my lymph nodes, and, at first, I thought it was nothing. When I went to the doctor's office, she felt it was nothing as well, but in response to my insistence, she decided to send me for a couple of tests, including a small biopsy.

The results would be in within a week or so, and we'd know what, if anything, we are dealing with.

"Focus, Sophie, focus," Savy continued to give advice even as he was walking away.

Chapter 5

"Sophie, I'm sorry to tell you this, but you have cancer," Dr. Beeman blurted out so quickly that I wasn't sure I heard him correctly. "The biopsy results confirmed this."

As the doctor said those words, I sat there confused. I am certain Dr. Beeman noticed the dumbfounded look at my face, and I also suspect he had seen that look before with other patients.

In my mind, I was thinking, *"how could this be?"* I am young. I am only in my twenties. I am feeling great, other than this lump on the right side of my neck. I immediately thought of Benny. I wasn't sure what this meant for him and me. The unknown felt scary.

I realized at that moment that I needed to do two things. Firstly, find out what is needed to treat this condition, and secondly, focus only on the outcome that I desired, which is perfect health.

Dr. Beeman continued in a soft voice, "We believe this type of cancer is a form of skin cancer, and even though you have no exterior lesions on your skin, it can start under the skin, and it can spread to other parts of the body. I'm going to recommend further testing to determine if the cancer is isolated in one area or if it has metastasized to another area of your body. I suspect the lumps in your neck are secondary, which means the cancer originated somewhere else."

Perhaps the soft, gentle tone of voice from the doctor was a way to soften the blow of the news, but I felt a complete sense of disbelief well up within me.

The doctor continued in a matter-of-fact way, "There are several small tumors in your neck. Even though there is a lump protruding out of the right side of your neck, underneath, there are four additional tumors on both the right side and the left side. Our next step includes further testing to determine the source and to understand if cancer has spread to any other parts of your body. Your case is being transferred over to the cancer clinic at the General Hospital, and a team of oncologists will be assigned to you."

As I left the doctor's office, I felt somewhat numb. I decided I would deal with it and follow the recommendations of the doctors. I knew I would get through this. I knew that my responsibility was to focus on perfect health, to feel healthy, and be healthy regardless of what was going on. After all, Savy taught me to focus only on the outcomes that I desired.

I had known many people who received a life-altering diagnosis, and yet they went on to overcome the odds. I would do the same. In one way, I found it odd that I was strangely calm, but I felt it was the positive conditioning that I had worked on over the years by maintaining a positive mental attitude and outlook on life and practicing principles of success.

Instantly I had a flashback to a conversation with Savy from years earlier where he said, "Sophie, no amount of studying, listening to audios, watching videos, or reading books on the subject of success is going to bring you anything or make a difference unless and until you *understand* it and *apply* it."

Because of Savy's teaching, I had become disciplined and applied success principles in my life every single day, and I never missed a day.

Studying success had become an obsession for me, albeit a healthy one. If Savy recommended a book, I would not only read it, but I would devour it and study it over and over until I became one with the information. As Savy suggested, I studied like a scientist and applied as I was learning. My results consistently demonstrated the positive attitude that I developed. Many people sought me for answers or guidance. So, in addition to being an author and teacher, I had also become a success mentor for others, and I loved every minute of it. My career was a rewarding career. I realized I could apply everything I had learned about being successful at business to being successful at healing.

After I returned home from my visit to the doctor's office, I decided to call Savy.

Savy was a busy man, but he told me to call him any time and for any reason, even if it was to simply say, "Hello." The moment I got home, I dialed Savy's number and began to feel a sudden well of panic come over me. The reality of what was happening was settling in. I was allowing the diagnosis to scare me. Unexpectedly, I was feeling extreme fear.

Savy answered in his usual enthusiastic style. "Hi, this is Savy, how may I serve?"

Before I could utter a word, I found myself in tears. "Hey," I managed to say through the tears. I attempted to sound calm, but it wasn't working. Savy was way too smart not to recognize the upset in my voice.

"Sophie? What's going on? Tell me."

"Remember that lump in my neck? Remember I told you that I was going to the hospital for a biopsy to have it checked out? Well, I went to my doctor this morning for the results, and he has informed me it is cancerous," I cried.

In a gentle yet stern voice, Savy responded, "You are crying over something that you don't even have all of the information for. You are getting way ahead of yourself, and you are putting your energy where it doesn't belong—on fear. You must focus. *What would you love, Sophie?* You've heard me ask you that question before, many times, and it is more important now than ever that you focus only on the outcome that you desire, regardless of what the test results show. Please don't misunderstand me. I am not suggesting ignoring the recommendations of the medical professionals, but you are in control of your thoughts and feelings, and I strongly suggest you get in control right now, young lady!"

Savy continued, "What are you doing right now? Where are you?"

"At home. I'm lying on my bed."

"Get up! Get up right now!" he demanded. "Go into your office and write this down."

Savy waited as I walked down the hallway to where my office was located in my home. I sat down at my desk and said, "Okay, I'm now in my office, pen in hand, and ready to write."

I knew enough to follow his instructions. Every time Savy suggested that I do something, I followed through. His advice always produced amazing results. This man knew what he was talking about. He was a self-made billionaire who came from nothing and created success in every area of his life. His results spoke for themselves.

"Ready?" he asked.

"Yes, ready."

"Write this statement down: *I am so happy and so grateful that there is only perfect health in every part of my body. I choose to mentally move from my head to my toes setting up a positive healthy vibration. Every molecule of my body is vibrating in perfect harmony with all the good I desire. It is so. Thank you.*"

I wrote down every word.

"Now, I want you to put that statement somewhere visible so that you see it every day. Perhaps leave it on your desk or tape it to the keyboard on your computer. But here's the most important part: when you *read it, feel it*. Feel the result with every ounce of your being regardless of what is going on. You can use this statement to switch from negative to positive, out of fear and back into faith. And remember, I am here for you. As you go through this next phase of your life, look for the blessings. In every adversity, there is a seed of greatness. It may not seem like it at the time, but believe me, there are going to be many great and valuable blessings and lessons to come out of this experience."

I wrote down, "Great and valuable blessings and lessons come from this experience."

"Everything that you have created in your life, Sophie, from your dream home to your best-selling book, and building a very successful, thriving business, all came because of your effort. You know how to get the results you desire, even when there is no evidence of it in sight. The same energy to create a successful business can be used to create a successful outcome with your health. It is a matter of desire, decision, focus, and energy. You know how to do this, Sophie. I believe in you, and I believe in perfect health for you."

"Thank you, Savy. I am grateful for you," I said from my heart. "You are literally a life-saver in more ways than you know."

Chapter 6

Within a week of being in Dr. Beeman's office, the oncology team (a radiologist, chemotherapy doctor, and a surgeon) were assigned to my case, and appointments were booked for a CT scan and an MRI. The initial appointment with the oncology team was scheduled for several days after all the test results were completed.

The waiting and the unknown were my greatest challenges. Constant negative thoughts and fear entered my consciousness. I knew better than to allow those negative thoughts and feelings to linger, but I was dealing with an experience unlike any other. As fast as the thought would float in, or the feeling would consume me, I would change it by switching to a more powerful thought and feeling. I found myself doing this switching technique multiple times a day.

Late one evening, after the sun went down, I was sitting in the backyard by the pool. Benny came to join me and sat with me in silence. I was unusually quiet. Benny asked me what I was thinking about.

"Life," I responded. "I'm reflecting about how precious it is."

Benny said, "Really? That is what you're thinking about? What I see is fear in your eyes. So, tell me what are you really thinking about? And you can be honest with me."

"I'm dealing with some fear. The unknown is what is scaring me the most, or I should say, I'm allowing it to scare me the most. Since I don't know the extent of the cancer, I don't have a clear prognosis. I am unaware of what we are dealing with, and I find myself going to a worst-case scenario. I have never given much thought to my mortality before. The doctor put in requisitions for more tests to look for cancer in other parts of my body. He mentioned the word *metastasized*, and until I did some of my own research, I really didn't understand fully what it meant. If the cancer has metastasized and is in some of my vital organs, the prognosis could be dire."

Benny was a wonderful listener. As he listened to me share my innermost dark thoughts and fears, tears began to roll down his face. I realized my diagnosis was scaring him too. I was so caught up in my own fears that I didn't give it a second thought that this might be difficult for him too. We held each other tight, crying, and he promised me we would get through this together.

As he held me, he softly whispered in my ear, "I love you so much, Sophie. I am with you all the way. I am all in and totally committed to you. We're a team now."

"I love you too, Benny. You are the best part of my life."

I slept peacefully that night, knowing that whatever was in front of us was not bigger than the faith we had within.

The health affirmation Savy gave me was one of my go-to switching techniques. Following his advice, I would read that statement multiple times a day and fully embrace the feeling of perfect health. I would also listen to my newly revised and recorded Power Life Script where, in detail, I describe my wonderful, happy, successful life, including being in perfect health. I was in the habit of listening to my Power Life Script multiple times a day. Savy was the one who taught me the value of replacing old programming with new programming by impressing desired ideas, images, and feelings through repetition. I loved listening to audios, so this became my daily habit of listening to *me* talk to *me* about how wonderful my life is. This process helped me improve every area of my life.

The day came for the MRI. With every new medical appointment, I really didn't know what to expect as these appointments presented first-time experiences. I had never had an MRI before. I already had a CT scan and found the test relatively easy and somewhat painless, other than the needle to insert the liquid into my vein. I assumed an MRI would be similar, but I wasn't prepared for my reaction to the small space that I would be inserted into.

The technician came into the waiting room, where I waited with Benny. He asked me to follow him to get changed into a hospital gown and prepare for the MRI. Like the CT scan, they injected a liquid called *contrast* into my system.

The MRI machine looked very similar to a CT scan, except the hole was significantly smaller, and the length of the machine was much longer. As they placed me on the table to be inserted into the machine, the technician placed a small rubber emergency-type ball in my hand. He told me to squeeze the ball if I was feeling anxious or was having any trouble, and I would be pulled out of the machine. I remembered thinking, *what kind of trouble am I going to have? ... and why do I need an emergency ball?*

"Ready?" the technician asked as he backed his way out of the room to go into the windowed observation room.

"Yes," I shouted.

The table began to move, and I closed my eyes. My entire body was inserted into the MRI machine. I thought it would help to have my eyes closed, but once the table stopped moving, I opened my eyes. I looked up, and the top of the machine was inches away from my face. Panic began to settle in immediately. I was overwhelmed with claustrophobia. I shouted to the technician from inside the machine, "Please take me out of here!" as I squeezed that ball continuously. With that request, the table moved again, and I was outside of the MRI machine, and I felt relieved.

The technician came out to see me. "What's wrong? Claustrophobic perhaps?" he asked with a smile.

"Oh, my goodness, yes! I had no idea I was this claustrophobic," I replied.

"Your reaction is very normal. You are not the first person to panic, and you won't be the last."

"Do you have anything to calm me down? Perhaps a sedative of some sort?" I begged, hoping to be given something immediately.

"Yes, that is a great solution, but you would have to get a prescription from your doctor, rebook the MRI, and come back another time."

Scheduling these appointments was no easy task as the demand for the MRI machine included several months on a waiting list. I decided to suck it up and get it done, and as I was thinking that, the technician had an idea.

"How about we turn your body around on the table so that your head is at this end, and once you are inserted, you'll be able to tip your head back and see outside of the machine. We are only doing an MRI of your head and neck, so that will give us what we need and help you deal with being inside the machine." He asked if that would work.

"Absolutely!" I replied with relief.

I got off the table and jumped back on, facing the opposite direction, and they put me back in the MRI. It was perfect. I was able to tilt my head back slightly, and I could see the ceiling of the room rather than the small space of the MRI.

Once the tests were completed, I was scheduled to meet with my oncology team. They would provide me with a plan of treatment. The first meeting was with an oncology doctor who specialized in radiology along with the oncology doctor who specialized in surgery. The chemotherapy oncologist didn't attend this meeting. At that point, I still had no idea where else the cancer was or the point of origin. Little did I know, they still didn't know the point of origin either.

"Let's start with the good news, shall we?" said the oncology surgeon, Dr. Paul. I honestly don't know what his last name was because it was an extremely long name, and I couldn't pronounce it if I tried. "Based on the results of your CT scan and the MRI, the cancer doesn't appear to be in any of your organs. This is very good news."

"Phew!" I responded. It was the only word that came to mind.

Dr. Paul continued, "However, we still don't know the source. We don't know where this cancer originated, but we have some suspicions."

At that point, the oncology radiologist, Dr. Lee, chimed in. "Would you mind if we put a scope up your nose, Sophie?"

"Sure, do what you need to do. Will it hurt?" I asked.

"It might not be pleasant," was her reply.

Benny was allowed to be in the exam room with me and sat directly beside me. As she began to insert the scope into my nose, it was immediately uncomfortable and a little bit painful, and I grabbed Benny's hand. The deeper she went, the more painful it became. I think I may have been squeezing his hand a bit too hard because I heard him wince.

"I found it!" Dr. Lee exclaimed. "The origin of the cancer is in your tongue."

"Whoa! Really?" I asked.

Dr. Lee was a lovely, quiet woman. She was rather petite and appeared to be very young. I wondered if she had recently graduated from medical school, but she gave off an aura of confidence, and I felt comfortable with her. She began to explain what the treatment would be and what to expect.

"Sophie, the type of cancer that you have is very treatable with radiation only and has a ninety percent success rate. Chemotherapy doesn't really work well with this type of cancer, although some patients have found it helps, but very little. It is my recommendation that we go with thirty-five treatments of radiation."

"Before we begin treatment, I'd like to run one more test to confirm we have identified the exact location of the cancer. We will put in an urgent request to schedule you for a PET scan. Once the PET scan result is in, we'll move to the next step and get you prepared for the radiation treatments."

It also sounded like there was no need for chemotherapy or surgery. Somehow, I felt I dodged a bullet of some sort.

Two days later, I was back at the hospital for the PET scan. The treatment plan was in place, and the start date was firmed up.

Even though Dr. Lee said the treatment might be "unpleasant," I had no idea what her interpretation of unpleasant meant, and I soon realized we had very different interpretations of that word. This was going to be one hell of an experience, and I was in for the ride of my life.

Chapter 7

While I was waiting for the radiation treatments to begin, I persisted in working in my business and serving my clients, continuing to feel fine physically and emotionally. One of the things I loved about working in my business was that it was a good distraction. I found myself totally immersed in my work and thought of very little else during those working hours.

It was in the quiet of the night when I would feel most challenged to switch my focus and build my faith.

Often, I would wake up in the middle of the night, and when Benny was sleeping, I was alone with my thoughts. It was a crucial time to get out of my head. I asked myself this question repeatedly until I felt the answer wholeheartedly: "Now that I am completely healthy, how do I feel?" I would fall back asleep reflecting on those thoughts.

Initially, we hesitated to tell any of our friends what was going on until we had garnered more information. Once we had a clear picture of what would be involved in treatment, we knew it was time to let others know.

My parents, sister Brandy, brother Clancy, and sister-in-law Allison were all informed about the cancer diagnosis. When I told the family, they had a look of terror on their faces. Sometimes the mere mention of the word cancer causes people to go into a panic. Both my sister Brandy and my sister-in-law Allison pulled me into a group hug and started to cry. I knew it was up to me to calm them down. I found it ironic that I was the one with the diagnosis, and they were the ones who appeared to be somewhat freaking out.

This news was difficult for my parents to hear. They had already lost one child when my brother Braden died, and the thought of potentially losing another child was incomprehensible. I suggested they focus on seeing me healthy and living a long life and focus only on that. I told them that is precisely what I am doing and that I had no intention of putting them through any more pain.

I was determined to get through this. I assured them everything was going to be just fine. My confident response and faith brought calm to others. Speaking in a calm manner brought calm to me too.

The day for the first radiation treatment was upon us. Benny drove me to the hospital.

Since the cancer was in my tongue and neck, a special radiation mask was created. The mask looked like a hockey goalie mask with special marks for the radiation. I also had a mouthguard to place on my teeth for every treatment. The mouthguard made me gag at first. When I laid down, the mask was placed on my face and head and bolted to the table. I had to relax my mind and imagine everything was fine. Once ready to go, I would be inserted into a machine for approximately fifteen minutes a session.

It took me a few sessions to establish a pattern to calm myself down. As I was inserted into the machine, all geared up, at first, I felt a sense of panic come over me. I used my mind to calm myself down. I talked myself right out of panic into calmness with the affirmation, *I am calm and all is well.* It took a few attempts, but thankfully it worked. After my first few treatments, I felt like a pro.

Benny drove me to every appointment. He said he would be with me every step of the way, but I don't think he realized what type of commitment that would be. He never complained.

Benny would ask me questions. He was curious about the treatments. "Do they hurt? Can you feel the radiation going into your body when they are doing the treatment?"

"Nope, not at all. The treatments never hurt at the time they're given. The technicians always make it fun too. They ask me what music I want to listen to and are happy to change to a radio station of my choosing."

The radiation treatments would occur once a day between Monday and Friday and twice on Thursdays. That meant six treatments per week for a period of approximately five and a half weeks. I was grateful that I had the freedom with my work to go to appointments at any time. I felt so much appreciation for Benny's insistence to take me to every one of my treatments. I had several other friends offer to drive me, including my parents, but I loved having Benny with me.

On Tuesdays, right after my treatment, I met with the radiation oncologist, Dr. Lee.

Prior to starting any of the treatments, Dr. Lee told Benny and me the following. "One of the common side effects of radiation is fatigue. You can expect some unpleasantness with this type of radiation. I don't want to alarm you, but there is a chance that a feeding tube may need to be inserted if it becomes too difficult to swallow."

"A feeding tube?" I asked with fear in my voice. "What is involved with that?"

Dr. Lee gave a brief description. A feeding tube did not sound pleasant at all, and I found myself thinking about it far more often than I should have.

It wasn't until the radiation began that we understood what Dr. Lee meant by unpleasant. After the second day of radiation, there was a significant amount of discomfort in my throat. It felt challenging to swallow, and an unusual amount of phlegm began to develop. That evening I turned to Benny and said, "If it is like this after only two treatments, what is it going to be like after thirty-five?"

It wasn't long before my appetite diminished, weight started to come off, and it really hurt to swallow. My neck was swollen and red. My voice was also raspy and deep. I sounded like a man when I spoke.

I would make jokes about how my sexy voice could land me a role on one of those call-in sex lines. Even though Benny loved my sense of humor, he didn't find that comment particularly funny. I was simply trying to find the lighter side to all of this.

Dr. Lee said to expect to lose fifteen to twenty pounds. I had thought I would be different. I never believed in odds and often felt we could beat them. If Dr. Lee said something that didn't sound attractive or appealing, I would dismiss it. Maybe ignorance wasn't bliss. The side effects became very real for me, very fast.

Two weeks into treatment, I realized that I was going to have to stop working for a while. I was not feeling great. It became difficult to even talk. Fatigue set in. My energy level declined significantly. I had two incredible team members who worked for me, and they both eagerly offered to run the business while I took a sabbatical. I felt confident they would take care of things magnificently. I was so grateful for them.

I found it oddly comforting being off work, which surprised me. I was so in love with what I did that, prior to my diagnosis, I excitedly awoke every morning looking forward to my day. So, to take time off, and to feel relaxed about it, was a new experience for me.

When this cancer journey began, I ignorantly thought that I'd be able to work through the whole treatment period. I did ask Dr. Lee if I needed to be off work, and she said I definitely would need to take time off. My perception of the effects of radiation was obviously obscured because I thought it didn't cause any discomfort or any major side effects at all. Since Dr. Lee said there would be some unpleasantness, I just assumed that it was going to be a breeze. Little did I know.

Physically I may have been dealing with challenges, but I was still very much in control of my mind. While I was resting, I would close my eyes and go on trips in my imagination. I saw myself completely healed and enjoying life to its fullest. I believed I was going through a temporary situation.

Deciding this experience was temporary was based on another valuable lesson learned from the wise Savy.

Several years earlier, at the beginning of building my business, revenue was extremely light, and I felt a sense of concern. I had money in investments, but I didn't want to take it out. It was locked in. Cashing in the investments would come with penalties. During one of my conversations with Savy, he shared his own experience of growing his business.

"Sophie, when I built my business, it was somewhat challenging. We had lots of ups and downs. We would have periods of lack and no revenue coming in the door, and then we'd be thriving. I realized in those experiences that I would not identify myself as a failure or identify the business as a failure. Instead, we focused on this being a temporary experience and reconnected to the outcome of profitability. I once heard this quote: *Being poor is a state of mind but being broke is temporary.*"

Savy's wisdom kept coming back to my mind at the perfect time. Before I met Savy and started working with him, his way of thinking had not been the norm for me. I had to condition myself to think in a new way until it became a habit. It fascinated me that sometimes I was still dealing with old ways of thinking, and I knew this was something I wanted to explore further with Savy during one of our next conversations.

As my physical body was starting to take a beating, I would strengthen my mental and emotional muscles. I studied more than ever. I listened to audios many hours a day. Something inside me felt that this was going to be one of the greatest learning experiences of my life, strengthening me even more and giving me an opportunity to help others in even greater and grander ways down the road.

Every day I would ask myself what I was grateful for. I would be looking for the good. I would find the seed of greatness no matter what was going on. Inevitably there was always something to be grateful for. I found this practice lifted my spirit every time.

A few days later, Benny came home from work with a special mug for me. It said:

Good morning, Sophie,

I will be handling all

your problems today.

− God

I loved this mug and appreciated Benny's thoughtful gesture and gift.

By the third week of radiation treatments, I was feeling significantly challenged health-wise. I had no appetite whatsoever, and the thought of eating was unappealing as my throat was raw with pain. The oncologist prescribed pain medication, but in the beginning, I didn't want to take anything that would numb me emotionally. It wasn't long before I was extremely grateful for those pain meds.

Benny was extremely supportive. He jumped in and took care of everything around the house, including meals and laundry. He instructed me to rest and heal. I felt so much gratitude for him. My parents offered to help in any way. From time to time, my mom would bring a meal over. I wasn't eating much, but Benny certainly appreciated it.

An unusual thing started to occur around the eighteenth treatment. We would go to the hospital, I would have my radiation treatment, and then come home and vomit. I would vomit repeatedly. Since I wasn't eating anything, I began meal replacement shakes. The nurses noticed my condition and recommended intravenous treatments of fluids when I would go in for my radiation treatments. I was grateful for those intravenous treatments as they felt like an energy boost.

After my twentieth radiation treatment and another IV treatment, I couldn't keep anything down. If I drank water, I would vomit. If I drank a meal replacement shake, I would vomit. If I took one of the pain meds, I would vomit. I became very concerned. Benny became very concerned. I was releasing weight, and my eyes were sunken. My neck was swollen, and I developed third-degree burns from the radiation treatments on the outside of my neck. I was having trouble sleeping and felt exhausted.

On the day I was scheduled for my twenty-first treatment, I was so weak that I could hardly stand up. That day I woke up and immediately started vomiting and couldn't stop. Benny decided not to go to the office that day. I felt my condition was serious and asked Benny to call for an ambulance. I knew that I couldn't carry on like this, and I needed medical help. My body was depleted of energy because I couldn't hold down water or anything else.

When the ambulance arrived, they could see I was in dire straits, and they rushed me off to the hospital emergency room. I was immediately admitted to the hospital, and this is where the nightmare became a whole lot worse.

Chapter 8

The emergency room attendants put me in an isolation room immediately upon arrival at the hospital. They were concerned with my vomiting and thought that I might have a virus that could spread to others. Until they ruled out that I wasn't contagious, they would keep me in isolation. Thankfully Benny was allowed in the room with me. They took blood and urine tests and sent them off to the lab.

In less than six hours, they had the results and knew I wasn't contagious, and I was transferred to a private room.

I was hooked up to an intravenous line and was being fed much-needed fluids. They inserted a PICC line into my arm so that they wouldn't have to put a needle in me every time they administered my medications. I was taking medications for pain, inflammation, blood-thinning, and nausea.

I felt a bit more relaxed knowing I was getting the around-the-clock medical attention that I needed.

On the second day of being in the hospital, I was feeling challenged with getting enough sleep. Every four hours, medication was administered. My vitals were taken twice a day, and blood was withdrawn to run more tests daily. It was not a quiet environment as there were constant announcements on the hospital's broadcast system. I would hear announcements such as "code white on the third floor."

Fortunately, Benny bought me noise-canceling headphones and some quiet meditations. I would listen to those audios at night with my new headphones.

I began to take naps often. Napping would help me get the rest I needed in intervals. On the afternoon of the second day, I woke from a nap and found Savy sitting in the chair in the corner of my hospital room. At first, I thought I was dreaming.

"Savy! What a nice surprise." I was genuinely grateful to see his face.

"I came to see my favorite patient," he responded. "Benny is keeping me posted. How are you holding up?"

"Doing great," I replied, even though it was evident by my appearance that I wasn't doing so great. I knew the only answer Savy would accept was a positive one, so there was no sense in saying anything other than that.

The next moment, a nurse walked into the room. She was someone I hadn't seen before. She didn't look very happy. I wondered what was bothering her. She moved about in an aggressive way preparing my medications.

She turned and looked at Savy and looked and me and piped up and said, "If you don't stop talking, you are going to end up with a tracheotomy. And, if you don't start eating, you're going to require a feeding tube!"

She was nasty. What was the point of her walking into a hospital room and having that tone? Was she trying to scare me? She didn't say much else and walked out of the room after giving me my medication.

Savy and I looked at each other. We were both stunned.

Savy started to speak first. "Do not allow Nurse Ratched to upset you."

Savy calling her Nurse Ratched made me laugh. I remembered that character from the movie *One Flew Over the Cuckoo's Nest* who was a cruel nurse.

"I know. I know," I replied. "I do wonder, though, why did she mention a tracheotomy and a feeding tube? Her comments didn't upset me, but they are concerning. I'll ask the oncologist when she comes to see me later today."

"It's a good idea to be aware of what may or may not happen, Sophie, but remember to focus only on your desired outcome. Deny the evidence of the senses. Live in your mind where you are enjoying swimming in your pool or taking a trip with Benny. Imagine anything you want. You can easily take a trip in your imagination, and you don't even have to leave the hospital bed."

He was right about that. And, every day, I was doing that by listening to my Power Life Script and focusing. I would lay in the hospital bed with a big smile on my face with my headphones on.

The visit with Savy was completely enjoyable. Being in his presence was always an uplifting experience. His energy was so powerful. I felt so relaxed after he left that I fell into a deep sleep.

My hospital room was located on the Oncology floor. There was an oncology doctor assigned to this floor, and she visited every patient once a day.

When the oncology doctor came to see me that afternoon, I asked her about a tracheotomy and feeding tube.

The first thing she said was, "Who told you that?" and she asked in a very annoyed voice.

I told her it was the nurse.

She said, "They are not, in no uncertain terms, allowed to scare a patient like that. The probability of a trach is unlikely, but a feeding tube may need to be inserted if you don't start eating."

I hadn't eaten in days and was relying on intravenous fluids to keep me hydrated. I had no appetite, so eating didn't appeal to me whatsoever.

Later that day, Nurse Ratched burst into the hospital room once again and said, "We're moving you to another room!"

Benny was visiting me, and I looked at him in disbelief. I loved this private room. It was at the end of the hallway and was likely one of the quietest rooms on the floor. I asked if I was going to another private room, and she told me no.

"Pack up your stuff, and let's go," she barked her orders.

I could hardly stand up as I was so weak. Thankfully Benny was there to help me. Benny gathered my personal belongings and went out in the hallway to find a wheelchair. I was not able to walk more than a few feet because I was so frail.

The idea of sharing a room was completely unappealing. As Benny wheeled me past the nurse's station, I stopped to speak to the head nurse. I asked her if there was any way I could go into another private room. She said there weren't any available at that time. I realized I had to find a way to look for the good in this situation.

I was put into a room with another lady. This lady didn't speak English and was bedridden. She was moaning in pain constantly. I learned that she also had cancer, but it had spread throughout most of her body. She had cancer in her brain, in her lungs, and they suspected she only had a couple of months to live.

She was an ideal candidate for palliative care, but her family wasn't giving up hope and wanted her to be treated. I heard the health care workers talking about how it would be best if she did go into hospice as these further tests and attempts at treatment were only making her experience more painful and caused her additional discomfort. It was sad to observe. I felt so much compassion for this lady.

If I wasn't getting sleep before, I certainly wasn't getting any now. Even taking a nap became challenging. There was activity going on in our room all day and all night long. As my hospital roommate was bedridden, she wore a diaper. She had diarrhea and required a diaper change almost every hour.

The nurse pulled the curtain between our two beds, but that really didn't serve any purpose whatsoever. I could hear everything. I could smell everything, and it was very unpleasant. The odor was strong, and it would cause me to gag. I was taking medication for nausea, so that helped me not to vomit, but the smell was so offensive. I was completely exhausted after two days in this shared room from having very little sleep.

The oncologist told me that I would have to get back to my radiation treatments, and they would be taking me downstairs that day for the next round of treatment. I was not looking forward to going for a radiation treatment as I knew what followed: vomiting.

An orderly came to pick me up to take me for my radiation treatment. He transferred me to a gurney, and off we went. After the treatment, I was brought back to the sixth floor.

It wasn't long before the vomiting began again. The radiation treatments caused me to vomit excessively. Even the nausea medication wasn't helping. It was not fun, and I felt helpless.

I was at my weakest point. I had never felt so frail in my life. Benny was incredibly good to me. He would visit me every single day. He would help me get cleaned up after my vomiting episodes. I was so impressed with him. He was a gift from the angels, and I told him so every day.

There was one nurse, Nurse Ellie, who took a special interest in me. She really cared about her patients, and it showed. The moment a private room became available, she arranged to get me transferred. This time the room was at the opposite end of the floor, in a corner, and it was much quieter. It also faced west, where I could see the Bridlewood Children's hospital from my window. Perhaps things were about to get better.

Chapter 9

It was the sixth day of being in the hospital. The thought of *when am I going to get out of here* didn't occur to me because I knew I wasn't in any kind of shape to go anywhere. I didn't even ask when I was getting released.

I had settled into my private room. I was never more grateful for a private room than I was at that time.

Daily I was being transported down to the radiation room for my treatment. It was typical for me to vomit for hours after returning to my room, but now I was gagging when the mouthguard went in before I had my treatment. I was starting to dread the idea of having radiation treatment. I asked the oncologist if I could skip a day as the side effects were too much. Fortunately, she agreed.

That same day the oncologist came into my room to tell me that it was time for a feeding tube to be inserted. I immediately started to cry. It was the thing that I was dreading. Yes, I certainly knew how to manage my emotions, but they were out of control at this moment, and I was scared as hell. Being in a weak state didn't help my emotions.

They scheduled me for that afternoon to have a PEG (percutaneous endoscopic gastrostomy) tube inserted. I was told it was going to be unpleasant.

There's that word again, *unpleasant!* It seemed to me that my version of unpleasant and their version were two different things, and I was not wrong about that when it came to the stomach tube being inserted.

I was wheeled down to the Endoscopy Department on the main floor of the hospital. Within minutes, three medical professionals surrounded me.

"Sophie, we are going to take great care of you. In a few minutes, we'll administer a sedative. This will help relax you. Once the sedative has taken effect, we will take you into the procedure room and get the stomach tube inserted." The nurse seemed to be deeply caring. I loved the warmth of her smile.

The doctor then explained the procedure in more detail and said the strong sedative is designed to help me relax, but I would remain conscious during the procedure.

I liked the sound of a strong sedative but didn't like the idea of being awake during the procedure. I had a hospital gown on, several blankets on top of me, and I was shaking. I knew I wasn't shaking from being cold. I was shaking because I was scared. One of the nurses noticed and went and grabbed a warm blanket and placed it on top of me. The warmth of the blanket felt good. Minutes later, the sedative was given, and it wasn't long before I was feeling completely relaxed. The shaking stopped. I felt incredibly calm.

They wheeled me into the procedure room, where the tube would be inserted. They began the procedure by inserting a plastic mouth device that would hold my mouth wide open, so they could insert the tube. They turned me on my side. I may have been sedated, but I started to feel anxious.

Minutes later, they put the endoscope in my mouth and started to push it down my throat. I started gagging, choking, and moaning, and it didn't stop until the tube was all the way to my stomach. The endoscope had a small camera on the end of it. This showed them when they reached the stomach. They made a small incision in my stomach, and the end of the tube was pulled through. Once that was done, the gagging stopped. It was a horrific experience, sedated or not.

At that point, I had a tube protruding out of my stomach that would be used to insert the liquid beverage. When that tube was inserted, I had no idea how much I would appreciate it, and I never thought I would have it for five straight weeks.

Three times a day, I was fed through this feeding tube. It was wonderful to be getting these nutrients into my body again, but the vomiting was still occurring after the radiation treatments. It almost felt like the feeding tube was of no use since I would vomit the contents of my stomach anyway.

I asked the oncologist to stop the radiation. I honestly felt that I couldn't take it anymore. I've heard of chemo patients who get so sick that they must stop chemo as the chemo was literally killing them. I had never heard about that type of experience with radiation.

I asked the oncologist, "Is this normal? Is it normal for a radiation patient to vomit every time they have a treatment?"

The oncologist said, "I can assure you every patient is different. I feel confident that your body is responding well to the treatments, and even though originally thirty-five treatments were ordered, we can stop the treatments now. I feel the results will still be positive."

At that point, I had twenty-nine treatments in total, had been in the hospital for twelve straight days, and I knew I simply couldn't handle one more radiation treatment. Thankfully the treatments stopped. I felt so grateful to have that part behind me.

Now that the treatments were done, and I was being fed by a tube and starting to feel a bit better, I asked when I could be released. I was told that once I was able to feed myself and had no nausea, I could go home. Immediately I asked them to teach me how to feed myself with the feeding tube. I was ready to go home and heal.

It had been days since I had a good night's sleep. Every four hours, around the clock, a nurse was in my room. After the feeding tube was inserted, I was told that I had to sleep sitting up. I could not lay flat. I had never been able to sleep sitting up. I had never been more exhausted in my life.

Some nights I would lay awake and stare out the window at the stars. Sure, I listened to my audios, but it was also nice to be in the solitude of the darkness and relative quietness. Savy taught me the importance of being in the solitude of your mind. He once said, "It is the quiet mind that gets things done."

On three separate occasions, all in the middle of the night, I observed the Children's Hospital orange helicopter take off and return a short while later. I could only assume it had gone to pick up a child somewhere. Since the Helipad was right outside my window, it was loud and interrupted my thoughts. When this happened, I allowed my mind to drift and wonder who they picked up and what was going on in that child's life and their family's life.

I felt gratitude that there was a hospital that existed for kids only. I was grateful they had a helicopter to pick up patients quickly when needed. I felt an overwhelming sense of gratitude seeing the hospital from my hospital room.

Viewing the Bridlewood Children's Hospital also reminded me of Savy and his generosity with his money and his time. He donated millions of dollars to the hospital, and they had dedicated an entire wing in his honor. When I started my business, I decided to contribute thousands of dollars each month to the children's hospital too. When I started my donations, one of the members of the Foundation called me at home to thank me and to ask why I decided to make a monthly commitment to donate to the hospital. They asked me if I had a sick child or a relative who was in the hospital. I said, "No, it just feels like the right thing to do."

Savy often talked about doing the right thing. I loved that about him, and he was a wonderful example.

When Benny walked into my hospital room, his presence always lifted my spirit. Every time he came to visit, I would sit up and put on my best smile. I could see him staring at my neck. It was a mess. It was red, swollen, and burned. I was prescribed burn cream and had the white stuff smeared all around my neck. Of course, I had the intravenous line in one hand, a PICC line in the other, and another line in the top part of my arm for my medications to be inserted. Underneath my hospital gown was a tube coming out of my stomach.

"Benny, why do you come here every day? You don't have to. I appreciate you, but it isn't necessary. Plus, seeing me like this can't be very attractive." I had to be honest with him and let him off the hook if he wanted to skip a day or two.

"Are you kidding me? Not a chance. I'm here for the duration, my love. We're together through thick and thin. And, by the way, I find you always attractive, sexy in fact." He winked as he finished his sentence.

"Sexy? I think not," I said with a laugh.

The hospital's biggest concern was my self-care when I returned home. The medical team needed to feel confident that I knew how to take care of myself. They showed me how to use my feeding tube. They ordered all the supplies for my home care and had them shipped directly to our house.

After two weeks of being in the hospital, I was released. Benny picked me up and wheeled me to the car. I was still quite weak and didn't have much strength. After all, I had just spent two weeks in a hospital bed with very little sleep. I ordered a wheelchair to be delivered to the house because I craved being outdoors. I thought it might be fun for us to go for an evening stroll while Benny pushed me in the wheelchair.

I hired a nurse to come to our home three times a day for ten days. Benny thought this was a bit much, as he felt I didn't need that much nursing care. Benny took a couple of weeks off work so that he could be home and take care of me. In some ways, I think he felt that I didn't have faith in him, but that wasn't it at all. I wanted to be certain I was doing everything the proper way, from medications to feedings, and a medical professional, such as a nurse, would ensure that.

I was never happier to be home. To be back in our own bed. To be with my man again. To go outside and enjoy some fresh air. Twice we took the wheelchair out of the garage and went for a stroll. Two days later, I thought it was time for me to walk on my own. I started slowly as I was still feeling quite weak. It felt good to be gaining my strength back.

Much of my day was spent napping or lying on the sofa. I wasn't reading at all. My vision had changed. Everything was blurry, and reading wasn't possible. I was grateful for audios and would listen to audios for hours a day.

I asked the nurse to start weaning me off the pain pills, and immediately we cut the dose of the pain meds in half. I found that I didn't need as much pain medication. A few days after I returned home, I stopped two of the other medications: a steroid and an anti-nausea medication. Within a week, I was completely off pain meds and all other pills.

I was more determined than ever to regain perfect health as fast as humanly possible.

Two weeks after returning home, I got a phone call from Savy.

He asked if I was up for visitors, and of course, I said, "Yes."

"Sophie, we're going to create a strategy for you to regain your health and discuss how you will use this experience to serve the greater good."

"Sounds like a perfect idea to me. How's tomorrow for you?" I responded. "There's no time like the present."

"You're right about that. The Universe loves speed. Let's make it happen. See you tomorrow. How's 9:00 am for you?" Savy asked.

"It's a date! See you in the morning."

Chapter 10

The next morning, I awoke in great anticipation of Savy's visit. In one way, however, I was feeling uncomfortable about his visit because I knew that I wasn't feeling my best physically, and my energy level was extremely low.

My physical body had been through a lot, and even though I was now on the mend, it was going to take some time to fully recuperate. One oncologist told me it might be a year before I felt great again. I immediately rejected that idea and decided I would be feeling great by the time the holidays rolled around, which was in eight weeks.

Sleeping had become a challenge because of the discomfort in my mouth. Several times during the night, I would wake up, and my mouth would be as dry as the desert. The salivary glands were impacted by the radiation and no longer produced saliva. Benny bought a top-of-the-line humidifier and put it directly beside my side of the bed. Between constant sips of water and the humidifier, it helped somewhat, but I would wake up a minimum of ten to twelve times a night. I started taking naps twice a day. I had a morning nap and an afternoon nap. Those naps helped me immensely.

Regardless of the interrupted sleep, I got out of bed, showered, and made my way to the sofa.

The front door was unlocked, and I put a note on the door for Savy that said, *Walk right in, the door is unlocked.* Benny had started back to work and had already left for the office. I was home alone.

Savy's arrival time coincided with the time I was hooked up to the feeding tube. I knew that Savy would be walking in at a time when it wasn't convenient for me to get up and answer the door.

As usual, Savy was on time. He walked right in, took off his shoes, and joined me in the living room and sat beside me on the sofa.

"You're looking good. I see I have interrupted your breakfast," he said playfully. I observed Savy taking in the surroundings. He looked at the feeding tube coming out of my stomach and eyed the pole holding the bag of liquid goodness. "How are you feeling?"

"Better and better every day in every way," I replied with great enthusiasm.

"I hear your voice is still a bit raspy. Does it hurt to talk?" Savy inquired.

"Not really. The doctor told me that my voice would be back to normal in a couple of months. The more I talk throughout the day, the hoarser it gets. Mornings are best, but if I talk a lot during the day, by the evening, I have no voice left whatsoever."

After the initial pleasantries were done, Savy did not hesitate to get right to the business of mentoring.

"I have an assignment for you," he announced, "should you be willing to accept it."

"Of course. I made a commitment to you years ago that I would do anything you told me to do, as long as it was legal, ethical, and moral," I responded. "What is the assignment? I have my journal and pen ready."

"I love that you are always ready and keep paper and pen beside you at all times."

His praise stimulated my resolve. I had fallen out of some of the habits I was involved in before I went to the hospital. Previously, I would write in my gratitude journal every morning, read pages of affirmations, study every day, do my visualization exercise, listen to my Power Life Script, read my goal card, write in my goals journal. I had stopped doing almost everything except listening to my Power Life Script. That was a habit so ingrained in me that I would never miss listening to it daily.

I was hesitant to share my shortcomings with Savy, but I felt he needed to know, so I told him. I also told him that I hadn't been studying because my eyesight had changed, and I couldn't read as everything was blurry.

Savy jumped in, saying, "It really doesn't matter what you are *doing*. What matters most is how you are *feeling*."

I interrupted him. "Wait, what do you mean by that? I thought these disciplines were must-do daily activities."

"You see, this is where people get confused. They believe if they are doing things, they will get the results, but that isn't entirely accurate. *Feeling* is the secret to manifestation. It is in the feeling state that you create having. You must first feel like the person you desire to be, and then you'll have the things you desire.

I nodded at his words. I understood the difference right away.

"When you are feeling as if that which you desire is already yours, and you feel as if you are already the success you desire to be, then and only then will you have it," Savy said. "The doingness comes out of the *feeling* state. If you are emotionally connecting to your outcomes, you are effectively in a manifestation state. In other words, you are in harmony with the goods you desire. You are vibrating on the same frequency as your goal. This activates the Law of Vibration."

"This is so good, Savy. Great explanation. I love this. Thank you. I was feeling guilty because I wasn't doing the same practices as before and felt I was off track."

I had barely finished my last sentence when Savy jumped in. "Guilt is a useless emotion. It will not serve you. Simply recognize what you are going to do *now*, at this *moment*, and get on with the work. We cannot change the past. We can learn from it, but we can't change it. Feeling guilty about it doesn't serve you. It harms you because it is a disempowering and destructive emotion."

When Savy broke into mentor mode, he broke in a big way.

"Today is a brand-new day. You have a choice as far as whether you are going to use it for good or waste it. You, and only you, get to decide that. You have been and *are* a phenomenal student. From the moment I met you on the park bench, you have been a person who follows through. I had faith in you back then when I hardly knew you, and I have faith in you now. I see greatness in you, and I believe in you. You are a difference-maker, and I love that about you, along with several other qualities."

His praise meant so much after what I had been through. Savy always knew what I needed to hear.

"Sophie, I have a highly developed intuitive factor. I sense that you have gotten lost in the last few months. I believe this experience has changed you, but don't get me wrong. It has changed you for the better. I feel that. You've gone through a significant life-changing experience, one that most people would allow to bring them to their knees. Not you. You are one strong woman. I know physically you are healing still, but emotionally and spiritually, I feel there is a new strength that has developed, and you may find that your goals have changed. Am I accurate on that?" Savy asked.

I was surprised. How did he know? I had been questioning my life, my business, and my goals.

"Yes, that is exceptionally perceptive. You are bang on. I began questioning what I'm doing with my life and where I'm going. I know that I'm living my life on purpose, but I feel as if I have been playing small. I was allowing my shyness to stop me from showing up in the world in a greater way. My top goal, my stretch goal, was no longer inspiring me. As much as my *physical* body was feeling less-than, the *emotional* and *spiritual* side of me was stronger than ever. I was starting to feel unstoppable and more courageous."

I took a deep breath. "I made a decision to change my life purpose."

"That's fabulous. What is your life purpose?"

"Previously, my life purpose was to make a positive and beneficial contribution to the lives of millions."

"I like that. That is a great purpose statement, but what did you change it to?" Savy asked.

"Now, my life purpose is to make a positive and beneficial contribution to the lives of *hundreds of millions*," I declared with pride.

"You said it like you mean it!" Savy nodded with a smile.

"Oh, I mean it. I have no idea how I am going to do it, but that is my new purpose statement. Do you like it?" I asked.

"Absolutely! I love it. I have built my businesses to positively influence and contribute to other people's lives. Being service-minded is the foundation for everything I have done in my life. Hence the reason why everyone in my company answers the phone with, "How may I serve?" as businesses are all designed to serve in some capacity or another. I love the fact that you have identified how big that impact will be, and I am certain you will precisely do that. I see you making a positive and beneficial contribution to the lives of hundreds of millions. I also see you doing this with ease."

Savy's words meant the world to me. His belief in me uplifted my spirits. I was feeling a shift occur within.

"Wait a minute! You haven't given me the assignment. I am ready for the assignment." I waved my pen and journal.

Savy smiled.

"Alright, here is the assignment. Please make a list of the *valuable lessons* that you have gleaned from your most recent experience and write out how you will use these lessons to serve others. Any idea that comes to mind, write it down. Take your time. Don't rush through this exercise. This will serve you too. I will call you in two days, and we can go over your response. Sound good?" Savy asked.

"Sounds great. Consider it done."

I was very anxious to get to work on this assignment. Mentally I had already been reflecting on the lessons, but I hadn't put them to paper. I loved the idea of extending my reach beyond the lessons to consider how to use these lessons to serve others. Savy knows how to take things to a whole new level. He was truly a wise master, and I felt more gratitude for him than I ever did before.

"How did I get so lucky to have you in my life Savy?" I asked him sincerely.

With seriousness in his voice, Savy replied, "Luck has nothing to do with it. We create our own luck. You attracted *me* into your life, just as I attracted *you*. I stuck with you because you are a service-oriented lady. I resonate with your heart and your giving nature. I see me in you."

"That is the greatest compliment I could ever receive. Thank you. I look forward to connecting with you in two days to review the answers. May you have a blessed day. I love you and appreciate you," I said as Savy was putting on his shoes.

"Love you and appreciate you too," Savy said as his voice trailed off while leaving the house.

Chapter 11

When Benny returned from work, he walked over to me and gave me a big hug. Oh, how I love his hugs. I love how affectionate he is. We would sit and watch a movie and hold hands. When we went for a walk, he would hold my hand, or we would walk arm in arm. During all my hospital and doctor appointments, he held my hand.

Benny changed out of his suit into casual clothes and came to sit with me on the sofa.

"Did you have a great day at work, my love?"

"Sure did," Benny responded.

"Did you bring any work home with you?" I asked.

"Yes, I do have a bit of work to do, but it won't take me long. Why do you ask?"

"I have some work to do as well. Savy was here today and suggested an exercise to do. While you do your work, I'll do mine. Deal?"

"Deal."

I pulled out my journal and began the assignment Savy gave to me. I was excited to begin. I wrote the words at the top of the page: Sophie's Valuable Life Lessons.

One by one, the lessons I had learned poured out of me. It wasn't long before my list included seven items I strongly connected to.

*****

Sophie's Valuable Life Lessons

1. If you feel there is something that needs to be dealt with, deal with it immediately. Take action and do not hesitate.

When I first went to the doctor's office, I was told to come back in three months if the lump was still there. The doctor was not in the office on the day of my appointment, and I met with a nurse practitioner instead. She thought my lump was simply a swollen lymph node and possibly nothing to be concerned with. I didn't agree. I felt it needed to be dealt with, so I persisted and asked for further tests. Thankfully she complied, and everything was set in motion. When it was time for a test to be done, rather than waiting for my phone to ring, I called the booking center and scheduled my own tests. This sped up the process of getting the test results, and it also sped up the process of getting into treatment quickly.

2. Trust your intuition. Your intuition will always serve you and lead you in the right direction.

My intuition guided me throughout the entire process. I felt the lump was something more than simply a swollen gland. Following through initially led to an early diagnosis. The doctors did tell me they felt we caught the cancer at an early stage. My intuition guided me to get further medical help when I was vomiting uncontrollably. The doctors told me that I may have saved my own life by calling an ambulance that day.

3. Cherish your family and friends and let them know you care. It isn't enough to feel the love. Tell and show them you love them and do it now.

Many people take their loved ones for granted. I didn't think I took mine for granted, but dealing with this health challenge caused me to be more vocal about how much I care for my family and friends. I asked

Benny what he loved about me, thinking he would say something like "I love your sense of humor" or "I love your persistence" or something about my character. Instead, he contemplated the question for a moment and responded with, "I love how much you appreciate me." I told him every day how much I appreciated him, and I pointed out specific things.

4. Look for the things that cause you to feel grateful. There is always something to be grateful for in your life.

Since meeting Savy, I had become a more appreciative and grateful person, but the health experience took my gratitude to a whole new level. I was giving thanks every day. I brought special gifts to the health care workers to express my gratitude. I would express my gratitude and appreciation to anyone I encountered, whether I knew them or not. After I met Savy, I started a journal and called it my GIMY Journal. It stood for *great in my life*. This created a shift in my thinking, but more importantly, being grateful created a shift in how I was *feeling*.

5. When you feel fear, take this opportunity to switch to faith and courage. This can be done in an instant.

Fear became an emotion that I was closely familiar with during the last few months. Quite often, when I was feeling fear, it was the fear of the unknown. I felt fear when the lump appeared on my neck because I didn't know what we were dealing with. I felt fear when they shared the result of my biopsy and confirmed it was cancer. I felt fear when they said my neck wasn't the origin, the cancer was somewhere else, and we didn't know where it was. Every time I felt fear, it was an opportunity to switch to faith and courage. Savy taught me to "hold an idea with my will." The will is an important mental faculty. When you can hold an idea and give it your attention regarding what you would love, you begin to change the way you feel, and you attract to you what you desire.

6. Use your imagination to focus on your desires. You can go anywhere you desire with your imagination, regardless of what is going on in your life.

I would be inside a radiation machine, getting radiation to my face and neck, and go to a sandy beach in my imagination and feel the warmth of the sun. I would be lying in my hospital bed, feeling like death warmed over, and imagine I was at home in my own bed with Benny beside me. I would be driving to a medical appointment and imagine I was heading to the airport to jump on a plane to head to another exotic destination with Benny. Imagination is a great way to manifest your every desire, and it is a great way to create a completely different experience if you are in an undesirable place.

7. There is nothing you can't do. You are more powerful than you realize.

I went through an experience that invited solitude. I had hours of quiet time to reflect and think about my life. I realized that I was playing small, and there was so much more to do and so much more that I could do. This lesson invited me to change the purpose of my life from *I am here to make a positive and beneficial contribution to the lives of millions* to *I am here to make a positive and beneficial contribution to the lives of hundreds of millions*. I choose now to step into a greater and grander version of who I am and serve in ways that I never imagined. I am ready for the next chapter of my life.

*****

The first part of my assignment was done. I decided to reflect on these seven life-changing lessons. I thought about creating a poster with the seven items listed as a reminder. That led me to the next part of the assignment: *determine how I would use these lessons to serve humanity.*

I turned the page in my journal and began to write part two of my assignment. I wrote out the title on the top of the page and began to write.

*****

How I Will Use These Lessons to Serve Others

1. I will create training and affirmation resources for others to use: posters, reminder cards, books, audios, recordings, and more.

2. I will become a successful syndicated talk show host who only focuses on positivity, growth, contribution, and enlightenment.

3. I will be a living, breathing example of these seven life lessons so others would benefit from observation.

4. I will teach others to become advocates for these powerful, life-changing messages.

5. I will create a new movement encouraging people to spread these ideas and concepts and reward them in creative ways.

6. I will use commercial media to spread the word of these life-changing messages.

7. I will create large gatherings and go to large gatherings as a speaker and inspire audiences everywhere.

*****

By the time I finished the assignment, Benny had finished his work and began preparing dinner. Benny wasn't a cook when I met him, but he became one out of necessity during my recovery. He became an excellent cook, and he seemed to enjoy it. From time to time, he would invite my parents over for meals. I wasn't eating solid food yet, but I would sometimes sit with them at the dinner table anyway. I loved how my parents welcomed Benny into our family and vice versa.

After dinner, while they enjoyed an after-dinner drink or coffee, I would lay on the sofa and observe them interacting. I watched them with such love and admiration. I felt like the most grateful woman in the world. My heart was full.

Chapter 12

Savy was scheduled to call me to review the assignment; however, I called him and suggested we meet in person again. He accepted my invitation.

The day Savy was to arrive, I wasn't feeling particularly well. Even though it had been a few weeks since I got out of the hospital, most days were still a struggle.

I was not sleeping very well, and my energy level was low. I was feeling highly emotional. The pain in my throat and neck was still very raw and real. Every day I applied the burn cream to the outside of my neck but swallowing something as simple as water still hurt. I wasn't on any pain medication as I had weaned myself off. The oncologist told me that the treatments and the medications would cause emotional ups and downs for a short period of time. She said not to be surprised if I became highly sensitive and possibly cried for no apparent reason.

I felt like I was on a bit of a roller coaster of emotions but quickly applied techniques to get myself back up if I slid down. If I listened to my audios, I felt great. Whenever I did visualization, I felt inspired. I was smart enough to know how to switch my emotions and became very aware of any downward shifts in emotional energy. When I felt my emotions heading in a negative direction, I immediately snapped myself out of it.

These types of emotional switching techniques were things I had developed many years earlier when I first began working with Savy. At the advice of Savy, I conditioned myself to feel good almost all the time. It had been years since I felt any kind of real negative feelings, but here I was feeling emotionally challenged.

I decided I would do my best to ensure I was in a positive frame of mind when Savy arrived. I listened to some audios and my Power Life Script, and by the time Savy arrived, I was feeling energized.

When Savy arrived, we got right down to business. Savy wasn't one for small talk. He also loved being productive, and he did not waste time. He felt time was a limited resource that shouldn't be squandered. One time he said, "There is an abundance of money, and money is meant to circulate. But, time is a precious commodity, and we don't know how much of it we have, so don't waste it." I respected him for that, and therefore, respected his time.

I was so excited to share the results of the assignment with him and dove right in. "Savy, the assignment you gave me inspired some new ideas."

"Okay, show me what you have."

I shared aloud my answers to the assignment while he attentively listened. He smiled, nodded his head with approval, raised his eyebrows, and leaned in as if he wanted to hear more. I loved the way he listened. When he was with you, he was completely present. I learned how to be more present with others by simply observing him.

When I finished, he spoke.

"I absolutely love this! This is valuable. I know this will serve you and serve others. I didn't realize you wanted to be a talk show host, though. That idea pleasantly surprised me, although I can see that for you. I believe you'd make a great talk show host. Did you know that I am on the board of directors for the largest television station in the country? If you are serious about being a talk show host, I can make some introductions."

I sat in stunned silence as I wasn't sure what to say. I felt a bit of a tug-o-war going on inside. Part of me was jumping up and down with excitement, and the other part of me was freaking out. Savy, with his perceptive sense, picked up on my emotions.

"I will make the introductions when you are ready. I understand that you are still being fed through a tube, and you have a few more weeks or possibly months of healing to do. But when you are ready, I will do a proper introduction. In the meantime, expand on that idea by coming up with a name for the show and ideas for the content. The more work you do to prepare for the studio, the more likely they will respond favorably to your idea."

My eyes began to tear up, and Savy noticed it immediately.

He said, "Sweetheart, be easy on yourself. You have been through a lot. It is now your time to heal. I have a sense that you are wanting or expecting to be able to do more than you can right now. Would I be accurate on that?"

"Yes," I said quietly. "It's completely unlike me to do nothing every day. Heck, Benny is even doing the laundry along with making meals, doing the groceries, anything else that needs to be done around the house. I will admit, though, I love being taken care of but feel like I should be doing more."

"Allow people to take care of you. Allow yourself the time to heal. Once you are healed, there will be no stopping you," Savy suggested. "I am sensing a renewed strength within you. I believe this experience has changed you for the better. You may not feel that or believe that right now, but you will know what I am talking about in due time."

With that, I got up and gave Savy a big hug. "Thank you. I love and appreciate you so much. I am grateful now more than ever to have you in my life."

"I'm grateful for you too," he said as he stood to leave. "Call me when you're ready to talk about your show. I will be ready for you."

After Savy left that day, I went for a nap. When I awoke, I realized I had forgotten to ask Savy an important question, so I called. He answered on the first ring.

"Savy, I meant to ask you a question when you were here today. Would you mind if I ask you now?"

"Of course. Ask away," he responded.

"I am finding myself dealing with old emotional issues from childhood. I thought those old ways of being were replaced. Why is this happening? Don't those old thoughts and feelings ever go away completely?" As I asked, I wasn't sure I was explaining myself properly.

Thankfully he knew exactly what I meant.

"Oh yes, those are your paradigms. Your belief system. They will fight you until the day you die. You may have replaced them, but they are still a part of who you are. This is the reason why daily work is essential; however, I have some suggestions to make this effortless for you. Are you open to having this be easy and effortless?" Savy asked.

"Absolutely!" was my enthusiastic response.

"When I get home this evening, I will dig up a treatment that I created for myself. I used these ideas to establish my own beliefs and, as a result, created greater *ease* in my life. It is a list of understandings or truths. I created this more than thirty years ago. Reading it daily and *internalizing* the words changed my life. I believe it will help you considerably. I promise to make you a copy and drop it off to you tomorrow. You're going to love this," Savy said.

Once again, I was grateful for his generosity. "Wow, thanks. I can't wait to get it."

The next day, a laminated document called *The Easy Code* arrived at my front door in a large envelope. Savy had it dropped off.

A handwritten sticky note from Savy was pasted on the front.

My Dear Sophie,

Please place this somewhere where you will see it every day. Allow these ideas to permeate and penetrate your entire being. As you read them, understand they are truths, truths about you.

Love,

I began to read *The Easy Code*, and as I did, I felt a sense of calmness come over me.

*****

The Easy Code

- Your journey from consciousness to reality is easily accomplished with your intention. *I easily choose my intentions now.*

- The power within you to create is available every minute of every day. *I easily tap into my power now.*

- Choose your thoughts and your feelings to be only in harmony with what you desire. *I easily choose the right thoughts and feelings now.*

- Allow yourself to relax in the knowing that what you desire is already here. *I easily relax now.*

- Everything you desire is available to you, and everything you need is within you. *I easily recognize this now.*

- Recognize that you do not have to know how you will accomplish your dreams. Simply feel as if you are living your dream life right now. *I easily feel it now.*

- What you give attention to expands. *I easily focus now.*

- Go into the quiet of your mind and allow the Universe to guide you. *I easily allow the guidance now.*

- Your dreams will be your reality when you live in the assumption that your dreams are already fulfilled. *I easily assume now.*
- Expect to win. You are designed to win. You are destined to win. *I easily expect now.*
- Control your imagination, and firmly and repeatedly focus your attention only on desirable outcomes. *I easily see my desired outcomes now.*
- The Universe has your back and is ready to serve you at your command. *I easily acknowledge the Universe now.*
- Enter into the spirit of your dreams by connecting only to those emotions that reflect the joy of accomplishment. *I easily feel the joy now.*
- Make decisions as the person who is already the success you desire to be. *I easily decide now.*
- Where there is desire, there is a way. The way will be revealed to you. *I easily trust the way is revealed now.*
- The fact that you had an idea means it is already done. *I easily see it done now.*

- Choose to live in the joyous expectancy of the best. Every day in every way, your life is getting better and better. *I easily live in the joyous expectancy of the best now.*
- Success is a journey. Enjoy every part of the ride. *I easily enjoy the journey now.*
- Assume your desires are here now. Remember the power of assumption and use it for your good and the greater good of humanity. *I easily use the power of assumption now.*
- Your success is absolutely guaranteed. *I easily feel the knowingness of this now.*

Chapter 13

My stomach tube was finally removed, to my great joy, and I was rapidly healing.

One of the blessings of being home was having the time to work on expanding my new idea of being the host of a syndicated talk show. It felt somewhat surreal to be working on this as the idea literally popped into my mind only a week earlier. I was delighted to roll up my sleeves and get to work.

My intuition felt that I was on the right track. Since I created a new and expanded purpose for my life, having a popular syndicated talk show was a great way to potentially accomplish this vision.

I was entering into unknown territory with this idea. I had been in that space of *not-knowing-what-to-do* before when I had approached different goals: writing my first book, speaking on stage, incorporating a business, and growing a successful business. But this was something completely new. I trusted that everything that was needed would be attracted to me. I knew that a big part of my responsibility was to stay in the energy of seeing my objective as a success.

Savy suggested giving the show a name and creating ideas for show content. I decided to create a proposal for the network, something that would be so impressive that they would be salivating to enter into a contract and get the wheels in motion. Savy offered to review my proposal and provide any input. I got on with the work.

One of the pieces of advice Savy gave me was the following: "Essentially make the decision easy for the network. Make it easy for them to say *Yes* to your idea by making the show so compelling and well thought out that they are eager to get started with the production."

The first thing I did was come up with a name for the show. Something that would be catchy, that people would want to tune in. Many of the existing talk shows were called by the host's name; however, I decided to give my show a different name: *Destinies*. If the network chose to call it *The Sophie Show*, that would be fine too.

*****

Syndicated Talk Show

Name: *Destinies*

Host: Sophie Edwards, best-selling author, speaker, mentor, entrepreneur, and business owner

Synopsis: *Destinies* is a daytime television talk show created and hosted by its creator, Sophie Edwards. The show features a diverse mix of fascinating and entertaining stories of everyday people who have overcome obstacles and achieved extraordinary results, providing constant inspiration for the viewers. *Destinies* is a feel-good show with special guest interviews and audience participation.

Target audience: Primarily women 25 to 54 years of age.

Objective: Be the number-one, award-winning, syndicated talk show in the world, with an audience of hundreds of millions of viewers and running for several years.

Airtime: The show will air Monday through Friday at a prime viewing time.

*****

Once the initial show idea had been flushed out, I came up with twenty different individual show segments. That part was incredibly time-consuming. I wasn't sure how many ideas to offer, but I assumed and imagined the show was going to run for years and be on television every day, Monday through Friday. Therefore, it only made sense to create a proposal with one month of show ideas.

It took a couple of weeks to complete the proposal. Many evenings when Benny and I were sitting in our living room relaxing, I would run my ideas past him. He wasn't the ideal target audience for the show; however, I respected and trusted his opinion. He also pleasantly surprised me with his fabulous feedback and additional ideas. He knew me very well and had additional ideas that I felt were brilliant.

Even though my proposal was in good shape, I decided not to call Savy just yet. I chose to reflect on the proposal for a few more days and expand on it or modify it if I felt something would make it more impactful.

Another week passed, more adjustments were made, and I felt the proposal was ready for Savy's feedback, so I gave him a call and scheduled an appointment.

We scheduled a time to meet the following day. I loved how available he was to me. He was semi-retired, and between his golf games, and the different boards he was on, he was a lot more available than he ever was. I was grateful for that.

When Savy showed up for our meeting, I handed him the proposal printed out on top-quality linen paper and presented in a beautiful portfolio. It had a look of quality and class. Once again, I reflected on the reminder from Savy that "you get one chance to make a first impression," and I decided to give a great impression with this proposal. It was important to me to impress both Savy and the studio.

"Truly, Sophie, from first appearances, you have outdone yourself with the presentation of the proposal. It looks like a top-notch, first-class proposal. Way to go," Savy said with such pleasure.

He hadn't read it yet, but he was already impressed with the first glance. I believe I made a great first impression and felt proud. We sat down together at the kitchen table.

Savy quietly reviewed the contents. In silence, I watched him with great anticipation. I saw him smile, nod his head, tilt his head, make affirmative noises, and open his eyes wide from time to time. He looked like he was enjoying the read.

When he finished reviewing the proposal, he placed it on the table and turned to face me. It appeared as if he was choosing his words carefully.

He began, "I can see this show being a big success. I do have a couple of minor suggestions and will write them down and send them to you. I would be honored to present this to the board of the television network for their consideration. I honestly believe you are onto an idea that could not only change your life but positively uplift and change the world. The timing couldn't be better as well. I believe the world is ready for this type of talk show and a serious injection of positivity. If you are open to my suggestions, you can add them in, and if not, that is okay as well. It is your show."

My mind was in gear, but my mouth wasn't. I was a bit astonished. I wasn't sure what I was expecting from Savy, but I had to admit that I was overwhelmed by his reaction.

Savy continued. "Next Monday, I have a board meeting, and I am going to bring your proposal with me and get it into the proper hands. Would you be willing to make a couple more copies that I can take with me? I would like those copies to be as professionally presented as this one. And, by the way, I think they should call the show, *The Sophie Show*. I love the sound of that."

"Of course, I'll look at your changes, adjust as necessary, and have the updated proposal ready for you," I replied with such joy.

With that, Savy rose from the chair and headed for the door.

As I watched Savy pull away, tears began to roll down my face. I surprised myself by this reaction, but something inside me felt this was going to become a reality, and it scared me.

The fear was based on the success, not the failure. I was feeling afraid of how this would impact my life. After all, Eddie withdrew from our relationship because of my success. How would this impact Benny?

Being a success came with a lot of benefits, but it also brought along several challenges too. I had read and heard how success impacted celebrities, and it wasn't always positive. I realized at that moment that I was giving attention to something that I didn't desire, and it was important for me to get clarity around being a success and having everything in my life be enhanced in only positive ways.

I grabbed my laptop computer and began to modify my Power Life Script. I scripted a revised version of my life, including being a successful, syndicated, award-winning talk show host and how this role only positively uplifted my life, my family's life, and the lives of others. I felt a sense of calm come over me and smiled. I re-recorded my new Power Life Script and put on my headphones to listen.

As much as I understood the process of creation and knew how to manifest my goals, my intuition confirmed that the next chapter of my life was going to be nothing short of amazing. I felt it in my bones.

Chapter 14

"Today is the day, my love!" shouted Benny from the washroom as he was getting ready for the day.

"Which day is that?" I responded.

"The day you hear the confirmation that you are in the clear."

"Oh, yes! You are correct. Today is the day the doctor confirms what we already know to be true."

In my mind, I was already healthy. In fact, in the early days of diagnosis and hospital appointments, I decided that I was not going to accept cancer as a part of who I am. I chose for this to be an experience that strengthened me, filled me with blessings, and allowed me to serve others better. I truly had a first-hand experience of what it is like to go through a potentially life-threatening health challenge.

As Benny was heading out the door to go to his office, he shouted, "I will pick you up this afternoon at 1:30 to take you to the doctor's office. Be ready for me."

"I was born ready, baby," I said with conviction.

My days had become increasingly busy with my business. I was back to work. I was teaching, mentoring, and guiding others to create success in their lives. The success of my first book brought a lot of attention, and I was grateful for it all. I loved serving others. I loved helping people.

Before I knew it, it was time to head to Dr. Lee's office.

Benny and I were comfortably seated in the doctor's waiting room. I felt a little tinge of fear and immediately dismissed it, just as Savy taught me. He said to be aware of my thoughts. He said to pay attention the moment a negative or destructive thought or feeling enters my consciousness and then to switch to a positive or creative thought. It only takes *a little bit of poison to kill*, he had advised.

As Dr. Lee entered the room, she was carrying a clipboard with a folder. I assumed it was my file. She looked up at both of us and gave us a warm smile. The smile felt like a good sign. At least I interpreted it that way.

"Sophie, let's talk about the results of your recent scans. I am happy to report that all tumors are gone. There isn't a sign of anything in your tongue or your neck, and you are all clear."

"Music to our ears," I said with joy.

Dr. Lee continued, "You are not out of the woods, though. We need to monitor you closely. We will be doing scans on a regular basis, and I'd like to see you in my office every three months for the next year, and then we'll go to six-month appointments. The goal is not to see any sign of cancer anywhere over the next five years."

We were in and out of that office in a matter of minutes. There was no sense wasting any more of her time, as she had other patients to see.

Benny held the car door open for me. I turned to him. "Let's go celebrate, honey. Want to do something fun?"

"I have to go back to the office. How about we go out this evening to celebrate?"

"Sounds like a plan. Let's do it."

I found it odd that I wasn't feeling a greater sense of relief after hearing the results. I suppose I had already been feeling enveloped in the feeling of joy and gratitude, knowing the findings of the scan would be positive, so when it was confirmed by the doctor, I really didn't feel any different whatsoever. I believe that is what Savy calls *perfect alignment with the outcome desired.*

I called Savy to tell him the news, but he already knew what I was going to say. He, too, was focused on the same result.

Benny came home from work a bit earlier than normal, and we went to our favorite Italian restaurant. We had become friendly with the owners, Beth and Evan, and we had our own designated table next to the window where we sat each time. It was the same restaurant where Benny took me on our first date. We loved the food, the ambiance, and almost every time we went to that restaurant, weather-permitting, we took a stroll along the canal after our meal. This evening was no different.

After dinner, hand in hand, we walked the usual path along the canal. It was a beautiful evening, and the sky was filled with stars. At one point during our stroll, Benny stopped and kneeled.

"Oh, my goodness, honey, what are you doing?" I said as my entire body instantly filled with goosebumps.

He pulled a ring box out of his pocket and opened it. The most stunning two-carat solitaire diamond ring flashed before my eyes. My heart was racing.

"Sophie, my love, you are the light of my life. You are my sunshine. You are my whole world. I have never been more in love and never been happier as I am with you. I want to spend the rest of my life with you. Will you marry me?"

"YES, YES, YES!" I jumped into Benny's arms as he stood up. He placed the stunning ring on my finger. It fit perfectly. We held each other for what seemed like the longest time.

As we walked back to the parking lot, Benny said, "I spoke with the owners of Angelina's, and they are willing to allow us to get married at their restaurant. They will open the restaurant for our guests only. What do you think?"

"I love it. It is the perfect venue."

Benny and I decided to have a small ceremony on the patio and invite only our closest friends and immediate family.

We moved quickly to get things in motion. We agreed to get married in three weeks. Our families thought we had lost our minds, but we weren't looking for anyone's approval. Some people asked if I was pregnant because we were getting married so quickly, but I wasn't. Although, after many discussions, we both realized we wanted to start a family as soon as possible.

Benny came from a small family. He was an only child, and both of his parents were only children. He didn't have an extended family. His parents were divorced and lived in different parts of the country. His grandparents were deceased. He loved the closeness of my family, as he never had that before. I loved both his mom and dad, but we rarely saw them.

Benny had also been married before. He didn't talk about it much, and his marriage lasted less than a year. They were very young when they got married and quickly realized it was a mistake. It had been several years since he divorced.

With our wedding, we weren't looking to create a big event. Our only objective was to exchange vows and be married to each other. I bought a beautiful white and gold dress, Benny bought a gorgeous tuxedo, I ordered some flowers, booked a photographer, scheduled a clergyman to marry us, and we were all set. No stress. Only ease.

We got married on a Wednesday. It was the only day that the restaurant was available. As it turned out, everyone from our immediate family was able to attend. Our wedding day was a glorious, warm day filled with sunshine. It was more of an informal venue, which made it far more relaxing for everyone.

My sister-in-law Allison was my maid of honor, and Savy was Benny's best man. They had known each other for many years, and even though Benny worked for Savy, they were dear friends. We had no other attendants. When it was time for the ceremony, the clergyman invited Benny and me to stand at the front of the restaurant, and we exchanged the vows we wrote. It was beautiful and intimate. I cried. Benny cried. I am certain there wasn't a dry eye in the place.

At the end of the evening, I would take care of paying for the food and drinks. We planned with the owner that our guests could order off the regular menu—anything they wanted—and we would pick up the entire expense.

Once all our guests were gone, Benny and I sat with the owners, Beth and Evan, to enjoy a glass of champagne. I asked them for the tally and took out a credit card. Evan said, "It's already been taken care of."

"What? That can't be. The total must have been several thousand dollars. Who in the world would . . . ." My voice trailed off as I figured out who paid for our wedding. It was Savy. Savy was the most generous person I knew. Of course, it was Savy. He once told me that he saw me as a daughter, and even though I had a close relationship with my own father, Savy and I had a beautiful connection. He also loved Benny.

"Let's get home, Mrs. Savoie, so we can start working on expanding our family," Benny said as he winked at me.

"Mrs. Savoie! I love the sound of that. I will be sure to get things in motion to change my name."

"You don't have to change your name if you don't want to. It isn't necessary to me. I know we're married. You've already built a career with the name Sophie Edwards." Benny said those words, but I knew he wanted me to take his last name. I felt it.

"I appreciate the thought, honey, but I am Mrs. Savoie now, and I am proud of my new name. People will get used to my new name, and my next book will have Sophie Savoie on the cover, proudly displayed. It has a lovely ring to it as well—Sophie Savoie."

"Next book?" Benny asked.

"Yes, Savy told me tonight that they want me to write my next book. Perfect timing as we are about to go on a quiet honeymoon by the ocean. I will allow the surroundings to inspire my writing."

"Excuse me? Isn't a honeymoon designed for something else?" Benny joked.

"Yes, of course, but there will be plenty of time for everything we want to do."

Chapter 15

The honeymoon was magical and relaxing. We chose the perfect setting on the Kailua beach in Kona, Hawaii. Being beside the ocean, staying in a spectacular villa, was therapeutically healing as well. We walked every day, read books, swam, went cycling, and enjoyed the many restaurants in the nearby town. I loved waking up knowing I was married to this wonderful man. It felt so right.

Once we returned home, it was back to business as usual. Benny returned to work, and I dove right back into my business.

Savy called to tell me he finally presented the updated proposal for my daytime talk show idea to the board of directors for the television station. He was originally scheduled to present during the previous month's board meeting, but the meeting ended up being canceled. The timing wasn't the best anyway, with our wedding and honeymoon.

"The board loves the idea and suggested a meeting with you, the producer of their top show, and the head of the network. They are serious, Sophie. If they love you, they did say that they'll schedule to shoot a pilot episode. I've arranged for this meeting to occur at 1:00 pm Friday next week. Does that work for you?"

"Yes, of course. What do I need to do to prepare or bring with me?" I inquired.

"Bring an extra couple of copies of your proposal, please. They copied the proposals I brought and distributed them accordingly. However, bring along a couple more. Also, be ready to answer any questions and make sure you look your best. Dress professionally. Walk in there like you are the success that you desire to be."

"There is one small change that I made to the proposal," I told Savy.

"What change did you make?"

"My name. Instead of Sophie Edwards, my name is now Sophie Savoie. I love the sound of my new name."

"Yes, you are accurate about that. Sophie Savoie rolls off the tongue. Remember when I said I loved the idea of the show being called *The Sophie Show*? *The Sophie Savoie Show* also works."

As soon as we hung up the phone, I called my hairdresser and the nail salon and booked appointments for the following Friday morning. I also blocked off time to go shopping for a new outfit. My intention was to walk in there looking like a million bucks.

I found myself feeling nervous about the upcoming meeting with the network. I would float from confidence to insecurity several times a day. I studied the proposal every day so that every show idea was at the top of my mind. If anyone asked me a question about anything to do with the show, I was ready.

Savy decided to go with me to the meeting. Having him with me felt more calming. He had such a calm, confident manner, and he positively influenced me. I watched the way he moved and held himself and modeled him.

We arrived fifteen minutes before the scheduled meeting. The receptionist escorted us into the boardroom. Savy suggested we sit at the head of the table. He said it would show strength.

A few minutes later, the room was buzzing with the television executives. We stood around and casually conversed for a good thirty minutes. Everyone seemed to be pleasant enough. As the meeting was brought to order, the head of the network, Phil Goodman, complimented me on the proposal and said they were in love with the show idea. They felt the timing was perfect. He asked me how available I would be to shoot the first pilot.

"I'm ready now. When would you like to get started?" I responded.

"Great answer, Sophie. That's the spirit," Phil said. "I would love to start as early as next month. This will give us time to get a live audience organized, and you can invite your first guests. If you can be at the studio next week, we will get started. I am assigning Hannah Templeton as the producer. The two of you will get along extremely well. She'll advise you on how to prepare as host and how to properly prepare your guests too."

I turned and nodded my head in Hannah's direction. I was conversing with her before the meeting came to order, and I really liked her personality. She was bubbly and sweet. As Phil continued, Hannah slid her business card over to me, and I did the same in return.

"We will get our advertising team involved as well. If the pilot is a success, we'll shoot a second show and a third. We will do a first run on a local network and then pitch it to others. This show could be an enormous success, or it could be a flop. We never know how the audience and viewers will respond. Ultimately, they call the shots. If people love the show, it has the potential to be a hit. However, if they don't love it, for any reason, it can flop like a deflated balloon. We believe in the show idea and feel it has potential. Let's see how this all unfolds, shall we?"

And with that, the meeting was concluded.

To say I was stunned was a bit of an understatement. I half expected to be answering question after question. I thought I would have to explain why I came up with show segments, but they seemed to be trusting my suggestions and allowing me to go with them. As I was approaching the door, Hannah called out my name.

"Sophie, let's get together next week to get things going. Would you be available to meet with me

Monday at 12 noon? I will order lunch to be brought in, and we can have a working lunch."

"Yes, of course. That sounds great. I will be here," I responded, "Thank you."

As Savy and I got into the limo (he always traveled by limo), I turned to him with a look of disbelief on my face. He was a great mind reader too.

"It is all going to work out perfectly, Sophie. Have faith. They fell in love with you the moment they laid eyes on you. Are you aware that they will also be assigning a make-up artist, a hairstylist, and a wardrobe person to you?"

"I had no idea. This show was only an idea that originated a couple of months ago, and here we are as it is turning into reality. Aren't you surprised at how fast this is all happening? I am."

"Sometimes things happen faster than expected, but that is rare. It is far more typical for people to underestimate how long it is going to take to manifest something into reality. There is a gestation period for all ideas to manifest into form. The challenge is that we don't know how long that gestation period is. In this case, it seems to be quick. I have another suggestion for you. You want to be ready for that first filming, so I suggest you watch the top talk show hosts and notice how they conduct themselves. Watch the masters. Observe how they hold themselves, their body language, and practice at home. You can invite a girlfriend or your sister over and pretend they are a guest on your show. The more you are prepared, the better it will go."

"Say no more, Savy. I have already been studying the top talk shows. I am now a regular viewer. I have been taking copious amounts of notes. I hadn't thought about doing a pretend or simulated show in my own living room to practice. I sure do like that idea. Great suggestion. Thank you. Thank you for everything. If it wasn't for you, this meeting wouldn't have even happened."

"My pleasure. The driver is going to drop me off at the office before he takes you home unless you would like to come in and say hello to your husband?"

"That's okay. I'll see Benny at home this evening. I have work to do and don't want to delay another minute."

Savy got out of the limo, and the driver brought me home. I walked into the house and sat down on the living room sofa. I reflected on what had just happened. Did that just happen? Am I really going to be a Talk Show Host? Do they really love my idea? The feeling of doubt was upon me, once again. In that instant, a powerful quote Savy had shared with me came to mind: *Act as if it were impossible to fail.*

As much as I was excited about this idea coming to fruition, I also thought about how much Benny and I wanted to start our family. How is it going to go with a pregnant talk show host? Probably not well. Maybe starting a family would have to be put on the back burner for a while. I decided to talk with Benny when he returned home to ask how he felt about it.

Chapter 16

The month leading up to the pilot was busy. I arranged for two guests to appear on my first show, and they both have powerful stories of transformation. I believe the audience will love the guests I chose and be inspired by their stories.

One of these stories is about a young man who had an accident while playing football in high school. He was blindsided while on the field and the impact severed his spine. The medical professionals told him he would never walk again. His determination and willpower proved them wrong. He not only went on to walk, but he now runs in marathons and ironman competitions. Inspiring!

We practiced many mock shows before the day of the live filming. My guests were prepped and ready to go. I was ready and confident.

My show producer, Hannah, and I got along like we had known each other all our lives. It turned out that we went to the same high school, although she graduated years before me. She was easy to work with and truly an outstanding producer. She groomed me for my role.

I simply didn't have the time for my business, and so my two team members were back to running things. Frankly, they did a great job. My courses were all pre-recorded, and they were assigned to customer care, marketing, and promotion. My private mentoring services were no longer available, which gave me the opportunity to devote all my time to the show.

My publisher wanted me to write a second book, but I asked that we put that off for several months. There simply wasn't available time to dedicate to writing while I was getting organized for the talk show.

I had a front-row seat to observe how a network ran its operation. It fascinated me. It was exciting yet serious. It seemed like organized chaos from time to time, but when it was time for the cameras to roll, everyone knew their place.

The day of the filming for the pilot arrived. My guests showed up on time. Hair, makeup, and wardrobe did their thing to get me ready. They decided to call the show *Destinies with Host Sophie Savoie*. The set was amazing. The word DESTINIES appeared in big block letters across the entire stage. The colors were vibrant and beautiful. They hired a songwriter to create a theme song for the show, and it was uplifting.

Everyone was in their place. I was seated on the set, ready to go. Cameras were set up from a variety of angles. The lights were beaming on me, and it was warm. The make-up artist came running out from behind the curtain to put more powder on my face. It felt as if I had two inches of make-up on already. I didn't usually wear much make-up, so that was one thing I would have to get accustomed to.

"Action!"

That was my cue.

"Hi, I'm Sophie Savoie. Welcome to *Destinies!*"

And the show was off and running. We had a live studio audience, and that brought so much energy into the room. Benny sat in the front row. At first, I was a little nervous that Benny was there, but when I glanced into the audience and saw his warm smile, it relaxed me. It was fun to hear the applause and laughter.

Inserted in my right ear was a little earpiece so that the technician could speak to me from the control booth. It was odd to be speaking while hearing someone else quietly talk to you in your ear. Thank goodness I practiced this and already had the hang of it.

He would say things like "twenty seconds to a commercial break" or "coming back in ten, nine, eight . . . ." He kept things running like a perfect machine.

We were told to expect eight to ten hours to shoot one hour of television. That day it took us just over eight hours. The first show was a wrap. Truthfully, it wasn't an hour of television. It was more like thirty-seven minutes, allowing time for opening, commercials, and show credits.

My instructions were to get the additional show guests lined up. It was my understanding that we were only going to shoot one pilot and see how people responded, but they decided to get a series of shows recorded. The heads of the network believed the show was going to be a success and determined we should move forward.

Thankfully, I had already called the guests for the next week and had them all lined up. Being an organized person really helped.

A couple of days after the first show aired, Benny arrived home from work and appeared overly excited. "Did you see the billboard along highway thirty-seven, my love? Have you seen it? It is amazing. There is another one downtown too."

I wasn't sure what he was talking about at first. "Billboard?" And then I remembered. "Yes, a couple of weeks ago, there was a meeting with the advertising team at the network. They showed me samples of billboards and television commercials they were considering running to promote the show. I didn't realize they started to run them. That's great."

"Let's celebrate and make a baby," joked Benny.

He may have been playful, but I knew he was serious about having a baby. We had decided not to use any protection whatsoever, and if I became pregnant, we would be thrilled. We knew we would be ready. We would make it work with the show.

The talk show was keeping me busy every day. Even though we filmed Monday through Friday, I was still working on the weekends to get show ideas flushed out and researching more guests. It was taking a lot more time than I anticipated. I was thankful for an understanding husband.

Within a relatively short period of time, the show was a national show, appearing on networks in every major city. The ratings were strong, and the popularity was growing by way of word of mouth. The advertising contributed to the increase in viewers as well. Since the show was a success, it led people to my book too. Book sales were through the roof, and it wasn't long before I earned the advance back and was receiving royalty payments. More and more foreign rights publishers were coming forth to buy the rights to *Destiny Treasure*, and each of them offered advance royalties.

Because of the popularity of the daytime talk show, I was starting to get recognized at the grocery store. Benny and I would go to a restaurant or a movie theater or just for a walk, and people would stop me to comment on the show and shake my hand. I would observe Benny to see if any of this negatively impacted him, but he seemed to love it.

One evening after dinner, I confessed to Benny that I was feeling burned out.

"Honey, I am not sure how much longer I can keep up with this pace. Between the television show, my business, and the simple demands of life, I feel I am being pulled in too many directions."

Benny, being the calm, analytical man that he is, offered a suggestion. "How about hiring a personal assistant? You could hire someone who is willing to do anything, from personal errands to business administration to being a buffer between you and the many demands and requests you're now receiving daily. He or she could take a lot off your plate and make your life much easier. You can certainly afford it. I would venture to guess that the network might even pay their salary."

"This is the best idea I have heard in a long time. You are so smart."

"Of course, I married you, didn't I?" he said with a laugh in his voice.

The very next day, I ran ads for a personal assistant. Many people responded. After interviewing several individuals, I hired an exceptional young woman. She called herself Cece. It wasn't her given name, but she assured me we would never be able to pronounce her given name anyway. She was young and energetic. She became my right hand and would do anything asked of her. She would pick up my dry cleaning, take care of groceries, return phone messages, take care of my mail, handle all kinds of requests, and book appointments for me. She made my life so much easier.

Everything in my life was wonderful. There wasn't a day go by that I didn't drop to my knees and give thanks for my amazing life. Sure, I had a previous health challenge, but I got through it and felt completely fine. My energy was strong.

More and more thoughts of having a baby entered my consciousness. Since Benny and I were not using protection, I was surprised that I hadn't become pregnant already. I started to wonder if something might be wrong with me. Maybe the radiation treatments caused infertility. I decided to call the doctor and ask if the cancer treatments had any adverse reactions that might affect getting pregnant.

"Hi Dr. Lee, It's Sophie Savoie. Remember me?" I stopped talking because I realized she wouldn't know me as Sophie Savoie. She treated me when I was Sophie Edwards. She knew exactly who I was, though.

"Of course, I remember you. How can I help you?"

"Last year, I got married, and my husband and I would love to start a family. We don't use any protection, and I haven't become pregnant yet. I wondered if the radiation had any effect on my ability to get pregnant. In other words, are there any adverse reactions to having the type of treatment I had as it relates to pregnancy?"

"No, not at all. The type of treatment you had, Sophie, would not deter you, in any way, from getting pregnant. Perhaps you haven't given it enough time. You may want to watch your cycle for when you are ovulating. I'm not a fertility specialist, but if having a baby is something you would love, I have absolute faith in you. You are a woman who knows how to make things happen."

I knew she was a busy lady, so I thanked her for the information and hung up the phone.

Perhaps it was time to get serious about this baby-making idea. With that thought, I decided to discuss it with Benny and start to create a calendar monitoring my cycles to determine the opportune time to get pregnant.

Chapter 17

The thought, *be careful what you wish for,* came to mind as I was having lunch with Savy. We were talking about how crazy my life had become since the show became syndicated and developed into the top show in the nation.

Savy listened attentively, as usual.

"Savy, I don't think I can go on like this! My schedule is insane. I'm up every day at 4:00 am, head into the studio for 5:00 am make-up, hair, wardrobe, and then onto the set to film. There are days we are on the set for ten or twelve hours. The long days can be excruciating. I return home and flop on the sofa. And, we want to have a baby. I know, I know, maybe not the best time, but when will be the right time? There is never going to be the right time. Now feels like the right time for us."

I felt a little concerned sharing this with Savy. After all, he was the one who recommended me to the studio, and now that the show is the top-rated talk show in the country, I want to have a baby. I thought he might have been annoyed with me, but in fact, it was the opposite. He started to sound like a proud grandpa.

"My beautiful Sophie. This is wonderful news. You and Benny would make such loving parents. I look forward to holding your bundle of joy in my arms. Frankly, the show can do reruns during the time you are away or get a guest host for the time you are on maternity leave. Talk show hosts need time off too. You seem very stressed. Being stressed won't help you in any area of your life. You are very likely sabotaging your own ability to make a baby because you're already stressed out that you are not pregnant yet. Want some suggestions?"

I had no idea what he meant by his question. Is he going to make some suggestions for the show, for making a baby? What exactly did he have in mind as far as suggestions are concerned?

"Yes, of course. Please suggest away."

"If having a baby is what you both desire, start preparing for the arrival. Buy a bassinet, a crib, highchair, rocking chair, change table, car seat, stroller, baby clothes, toys, diapers, anything and everything you would want or need for a newborn baby. Decide which room in your home will be the baby's room and get it ready. Go to the maternity store and buy some maternity clothes. Act as if you are already pregnant. How would you feel if you knew you were pregnant right now with a healthy baby growing in your tummy?"

"Seriously? Buy maternity clothes? Get the baby's room ready now? Buy all that stuff now? Isn't that getting a little ahead of ourselves?" I was kind of surprised by his suggestion even though I liked it. I liked it a lot. It simply surprised me as it sounded extreme.

Savy continued. "The Universe responds to your emotions. When you act and feel as if your desire is already here, and you give this your dominant attention, you will make it happen. Right now, you are directing your attention to why you are not getting pregnant. You've done nothing to prepare. It really is this simple. Listen, these actions will demonstrate to the Universe you are serious about this. What is the worst that can happen? If you don't get pregnant, you can sell the stuff. However, having said that, I suggest you don't give any thought to having to sell it. Only think about what you want. Touch your belly and feel the baby growing inside you. Pretend the baby kicked. Life can be a game sometimes, but you have to know how to play it."

"Oh, now I understand. You are talking about the manifestation process again. It works on anything. I have no idea why I didn't think of this." I felt confident with his suggestion now.

"What are you going to call your baby? Stephen is a good name if it is a boy," Savy joked, as his given name was Stephen. I happened to love his middle name, Alexander.

"Benny and I haven't even discussed names, but this type of preparation for the baby is a great idea for the two of us. I will be sure to bring this up at dinner this evening. Thank you."

I always walked away from a rendezvous with Savy feeling uplifted. What a gift he had to see things the way he did. One time he told me that he didn't think in this manner when he was younger. He taught himself to think positively and to live in the joyous expectancy of the best. He said, over time, it became a habit, and now it is the only way he thinks.

Three months later, I became pregnant. I immediately started to have morning sickness. This concerned me, as my belly wasn't showing, and people at the network were wondering why I kept excusing myself to go to the ladies' room. We decided not to tell anyone until we were past the sixteen-week phase.

One weekend, we were lying around the house when sharp pains started in my abdomen. I called for Benny, and he came running. He looked down and could see I was bleeding.

"My love, you're bleeding." I could hear the panic in Benny's voice. "Should I call for an ambulance?"

"Honey, please help me get up. I need to go to the bathroom. Don't call anyone just yet," I pleaded.

I knew this wasn't a good sign. I felt in my heart that something had happened to the baby. I cleaned myself up and asked Benny to take me to the emergency room.

At the hospital, it was confirmed that I had a miscarriage. Benny and I cried. We felt such pain in our hearts for the loss. They performed a dilation and curettage, also known as a D & C, and I was released.

The nurse suggested that I go home and rest. She said I would feel fine in a day or two.

Since we hadn't told anyone about the pregnancy, we decided to also keep the miscarriage our secret. We were both sad about what happened and allowed ourselves to grieve. We felt that we would go back to baby-making when I had healed and when the time felt right.

Time has a wonderful way of curing all wounds, emotional and physical. It wasn't long before we were calculating the best time and days to get pregnant. Our spirits had lifted, and we felt confident we would become pregnant once again.

Sure enough, after doing a home pregnancy test, we were expecting once again. This time, there wasn't any morning sickness. In fact, I felt more energetic. I was surprised by how great I was feeling. I thought every pregnant woman had morning sickness, but according to my doctor, apparently not. I absolutely loved being pregnant. Having a baby growing inside my belly felt like a miracle. I had never seen Benny happier. I was never happier.

It felt like time was flying, and we were already at the sixteen-week timeframe of my pregnancy. I had a small baby bump. I didn't think anyone noticed as I was wearing clothes that were loose-fitting. We invited our families and a few friends, Savy and Carol included, over to our home for a barbecue and announced our news. It was a wonderful, happy celebration.

On Monday morning, I would tell Hannah, the producer. I honestly didn't know what she would say or how she would respond, but I was hoping she would be happy for me. The moment Hannah arrived at the studio on Monday, I would tell her.

"Hannah, can I see you in here, please?" I was already in the green room getting ready to go on the set. We still had lots of time, as I arrived early.

"Sure. What's up, buttercup?" she asked with a giggle in her voice.

I loved Hannah's personality. Every day she showed up in a great mood. Not everyone else on the set did, but I could always count on her bubbly spirit to brighten up the room.

"I have something to tell you."

"You're pregnant! Right? Am I right?" Hannah asked with a genuine expression of joy.

"Oh, my goodness, how in the world did you know?"

"You are glowing. You also have a little baby bump. I noticed that first. Your skirts and pants seem a bit tighter. I watch you like a hawk. Don't take that in a creepy way, but it is my job."

"You are very good at what you do. No denying that. Aren't you upset or angry with me? Are you concerned about the show?"

"I am thrilled for you. This is wonderful news. We'll find a replacement host for the time you are on maternity leave. You are coming back, right?"

"Yes, I'm planning on working throughout my pregnancy and returning to the show. I feel great, so there is no need to take any time off. I think our viewers will enjoy watching the growth of my belly. Should we make a formal announcement of some sort on the air?" I asked.

"Yes, let's do it. We can do it tomorrow. I will have someone write up the announcement for you, and you can review it, and we'll start the show tomorrow with the good news."

Having Hannah's blessing was a huge relief.

Hannah called a meeting with all the employees from the talk show team. The purpose of the meeting was to tighten the time it took to film a show. She felt we could cut the time significantly if we created a better system. I was in love with this idea.

Within a short period of time, we were filming shows in half the time that it previously took. This gave me the opportunity to enjoy more quality time at home with my husband and to be more relaxed. I was starting to feel the fatigue as the pregnancy went along.

Benny and I decided to find out what the sex of our baby was, so at our ultrasound meeting, we asked the technician to tell us if she could determine the sex.

As I lay on the ultrasound table, with the cool jelly on my baby bump and the ultrasound wand moving around, listening to the baby's rapid heartbeat, the technician piped up. "Ready? Ready to know the sex of your baby?"

"Yes," we shouted in unison.

"You are having a little boy! Look right there, and you'll see." She pointed to something that looked like an ink spot.

"A baby boy! Wow." I felt those wonderful goosebumps once again consume my entire body. We were elated to be having a son. We would have been just as happy if it was a girl.

Benny leaned down and gave me a kiss on my forehead and moved down to my exposed baby bump and kissed it. As he did, he whispered, "Hi, Benny Junior. This is your daddy. I love you. We will see you soon."

"Benny Junior?" I laughed. "Maybe it's time to have the conversation about what we will name our baby."

Chapter 18

A guest host had been organized to take over the *Destinies* show while I was away on maternity leave. He was a gentleman by the name of Leon Miller, and he was already a news reporter with the network. He had great charisma and presence. Leon and I had several strategy meetings to prepare him to take over. He brought valuable segment ideas, and I knew the show would be in great hands.

At thirty-seven weeks into my pregnancy, my obstetrician told me he felt happy with the way things were progressing, except for one issue. He said the placenta wasn't in the right place. He told me that he would be watching me closely and would likely need to do another ultrasound the following week. He assured me there was nothing to be concerned about.

One week later, Benny and I were back at the obstetrician's office for another ultrasound. I loved hearing the baby's heartbeat. As the ultrasound was being conducted, Dr. Daniel was quiet. He had a definite look of concern on his face.

"Benny, Sophie, we are going to schedule a cesarean section for the end of next week. It appears that the placenta is partially blocking the cervix. Don't worry. We've seen this many times before. It is safest for both the mom and baby to deliver this way."

"Okay, as long as our baby is safe," I said.

"Your baby boy is perfectly healthy. He is developing well. I estimate he is already over seven pounds. I will call the hospital and get this scheduled. Sophie, you will need to check into the hospital the night before, and I'd like to perform the C-section on Friday."

"That's Friday the thirteenth! I found out I was pregnant eight months ago, on Friday the thirteenth. This must be my lucky day," I announced.

Dr. Daniel was already leaving the room and turned and said, "I think it is a perfect day to welcome your son into the world."

"Wait! Sorry, just one more question, please. Will I be conscious when he is being born? Am I awake during the C-section?" I wanted to hold my baby the moment he came out of my belly. It was important to me.

"Yes, absolutely!" The door closed behind the doctor as he left.

On the following Thursday, I was scheduled to check into a private room at the hospital. Going back to the hospital brought back lots of undesirable memories from my cancer experience, but we were about to create some wonderful memories.

Benny drove me to the hospital. As we both entered the admittance area, I saw a familiar face. It was Carol, Savy's wife. She was walking toward the elevator.

I turned to Benny. "Did you see her? It is Carol, Savy's wife. What is she doing here?" I knew full well that Benny didn't know, or at least, I didn't think he knew why Carol was at the hospital, but I asked Benny to race over to get her attention.

Benny was able to move faster than me. He walked swiftly and met up with Carol at the elevator. I followed behind at a bit of a slower pace. As I approached the two of them, I caught Carol's words.

"Earlier today, Savy had some pain in his chest, and his breathing became labored. Savy isn't one to alarm anyone, but he did ask me to call emergency. We arrived minutes ago by ambulance. Savy is conscious, but they are going to have to find out what caused the chest pain and the shortness of breath. I'm on my way up to the Intensive Care Unit to be with him."

"Oh, Carol," I said with a quick intake of breath. "Please give him our love."

"We're here for Sophie's C-section," Benny told her, "which will be performed in the morning. We're checking in on the maternity floor, the fifth floor. Would you please come and find us or somehow get a message to us about how Savy is doing?"

"Yes, of course. Best of luck to both of you. Happy delivery too. I promise to keep you updated." Carol's voice shook a little when she spoke. I was praying Savy was going to be fine.

The elevator door made a loud ding, and we all got in and pushed the button for our appropriate floor. Carol got out on the ICU floor, and we rode up to the fifth floor.

Benny and I agreed that Savy was in great hands. We had to keep our focus on getting our son safely delivered.

The private rooms on the maternity floor were large, warmly decorated, and comfortable, unlike a typical hospital room.

After we got settled in, I turned to Benny and said, "Honey, it's just you and me right now, but in a few hours, we'll be three. I am so excited to finally get to meet our son in the morning. The doctor told me they are taking me down to the operating room at 7:00 am."

"I can't wait!" said Benny. "Want to talk about names for our son? We haven't finalized his name yet. We bounced around some ideas, but none of them stuck."

"My thought is to wait until we see his little face. I believe we'll know the moment we see him. How do you feel about that?"

"Sounds great, my love. You should try and get some sleep. I'm going to recline in this chair and stay with you for the night." Benny had already told me he wasn't leaving. The hospital allowed the fathers to stay with the mothers, so we felt we would take advantage of that.

The night nurse walked into the room. "How are Mom and Dad tonight? Feeling excited to meet your baby tomorrow?" She took a quick look around the room and continued, "Hey, Mr. Savoie, would you like a cot? I can arrange to have a cot brought into the room. You will be a lot more comfortable."

"Yes, please! That would be wonderful. Thank you."

Feeling somewhat fatigued, I decided to go to sleep early. In only a matter of hours, our entire world is going to change for the better. This also meant our sleep wouldn't be the same for quite some time.

We turned off all the lights and settled in for the night. Within minutes I was fast asleep. At precisely 2:22 am, I woke up with a jolt. I had been dreaming of Savy, and the dream felt so real. In the dream, Savy and I were back on our favorite park bench, the same bench where I met him years earlier. We were talking, laughing, and reminiscing. It felt so real to me, but somehow, I knew it was a dream.

As the dream was ending, just as Savy and I had done many times, we both stood up. As we leaned in to hug each other, Savy said these words: "Don't cry for me. I am in a better place." I tried to hug him, but he disappeared, and I woke up. I didn't know what his words meant. It was puzzling. Here it was, the middle of the night, and I was now wide awake. I started to wonder if this was a message from Savy. I started to question the dream and the meaning. My maternal instincts kicked in, and I knew I had to stop worrying over a dream and focus on calming thoughts and our baby.

I looked over at Benny. He was sleeping peacefully on the cot. I needed to go back to sleep as our alarm would be going off in a few short hours.

At ten minutes before 7:00 am, an orderly came to the room. He asked me to transfer to the gurney. It was time to be taken to the operating room.

Once in the operating room, they draped a partial curtain so that I couldn't see the medical team doing the C-section. Benny waited in the adjacent room and would be brought in once the baby was taken out of me.

I had been given a mild sedative, and when they were ready to perform the surgery, they froze my midsection. They told me they were about to open me up, but thankfully I couldn't feel a thing. Minutes later,

Benny was brought into the operating room. He stood directly beside my head. It seemed as if it was only minutes later, and the doctor pulled our baby boy out of my womb. Benny cut the umbilical cord, and they placed him on my chest.

There are no words to describe the immense love I felt seeing him for the first time. I was completely in love. Our baby was the most beautiful baby I ever laid eyes on.

Benny started snapping all kinds of photos. He asked the nurse to take a photo of the three of us. Benny had also installed a tripod in the corner with a video camera capturing it all.

"Welcome to the world, Baby Savoie. Congratulations, Mom and Dad," Dr. Daniel announced.

After investing a bit of time in the recovery room, I was brought back up to my private room. Benny was sitting in a rocking chair, holding our son.

I glanced to the nightstand beside the bed and noticed an envelope with a yellow note taped on top. "What's that?" I asked.

Benny glanced over and said, "I have no idea. It was here when I returned to the room. Read it, and the mystery will be solved."

I picked up the envelope. "It's a note from Carol!"

Carol's message was written on a yellow sticky note.

*****

Sophie & Benny,

I am sorry to tell you this, but Savy passed away this morning at 2:22 am. He died peacefully. He felt it was his time. Please find comfort in his words.

Love, Carol

*****

My Dear Sophie,

If you are reading this, then you now know that I am onto the next phase of my eternal journey. Please do not feel sad or shed tears. I am at peace. I will be with you in spirit, always in all ways. Think of me, and I will be with you.

I knew my transition was coming. My intuition guided me to write to you. I wrote this letter in advance and asked Carol to hold it until it was the appropriate time to hand it to you.

You have created a charmed life, and I know how much you appreciate it. Continue to shine your light in the world. There is so much more ahead of you, Sophie, and I know it is all going to be magnificent. You are making a positive and beneficial contribution to hundreds of millions of people. I love that you are in love with helping people. You are excellent at it, and the world needs you now more than ever.

You will heal where there is pain. You will bring lightness where there is darkness. You will uplift where hearts are heavy. You will fan the flame of weakened passions. Your work is far from done. You will be amazed and astonished at the great work you will do in this world.

You have already accomplished a significant amount in a short period of time. I am so proud of you. If I had a daughter, I would want her to be just like you. And, the love I feel for you is in alignment with the love you are feeling now as you stare into the eyes of your baby boy.

Love now and always,

*****

I read the letter to Benny. The dream made perfect sense to me now. Tears flowed down my cheeks.

There were so many conflicting emotions in a short period of time—I lost my cherished friend and mentor and gained a beautiful son.

I glanced over at Benny, holding our newborn son, and I knew, at that moment, the perfect name for our son: Stephen Alexander Vaughan Savoie. And we would call him Savy.

The End

Did You Love This Book, And Would You Like More Savy Wisdom?

Explore This All-New Online Program And Implement Savy Wisdom Into Your Life!

Learn More:
{ www.SavyWisdom.com/SPSP }

Does This Sound Like You?

- You Feel Stuck, But Know There Is More To Life Than You Are Currently Experiencing
- You Have A Burning Desire To Do Something Meaningful
- You Dream Of Upgrading Your Life
- You Care Deeply About Making A Positive Impact In The World

Then keep reading the following pages!

Experience The Power of Savy Wisdom™

You're About To...

Expand Your Awareness

What are you choosing to focus on? It's time to expand your awareness to the tremendous power deep within you. Create your own GIMY journal to effectively build paradigms that will serve you in only positive ways.

Discover Your Passion

What would you love? We were all given a gift at birth; the gift of choice. Create the ideal life - no more "tip toe-ing" through life hoping you will make it safely to death. Remember, you don't need to know the HOW.

Achieve Your Goals and Dreams

What do you need to believe in order to accomplish your goals and dreams? Through effective use of your imagination and creation of your own SABY journal, all you desire is already yours.

Live From The End

Get clarity around your passion and learn to look for the good in every situation. Through spaced time repetition you will learn to live from the end. Discover the power of living in state of gratitude all day long. This new found belief will be your key to success.

Move Into Action

There are many roads to get to your destination - learn how to choose the "right" road or the most direct way. Discover what actions will move you in the right direction.

Stay In Alignment

With magic when you know how it works, the magic disappears. With life when you know how it works, the magic begins. Learn how to stay away from the negative and how to instantly switch into the positive.

Learn More:
{ www.SavyWisdom.com/SPSP }

About The Author

Peggy McColl is a world-renowned wealth, business and manifestation expert as well as the New York Times Best Selling Author of *Your Destiny Switch: Master Your Key Emotions And Attract the Life of Your Dreams.*

She has worked with – and been endorsed by – some of the most renowned experts in the personal development field including Bob Proctor, Neale Donald Walsch, Jim Rohn, Dr. Wayne Dyer, Mark Victor Hansen, Caroline Myss, Gregg Braden, Debbie Ford , Arielle Ford, Hay House, Marianne Williamson, Dean Graziosi, Gay Hendricks, Marie Forleo and many others

Peggy's special, unique, and intensive programs, speaking engagements, goal achievement seminars, and best-selling books have inspired and instructed "everyday" individuals, entrepreneurs, authors and organizations to reach their maximum potential and truly take massive quantum leaps.

Peggy can help you to realize your success (both mentally, spiritually, and in the real world), whatever your chosen field may be! Whether you want to manifest a dream life, build your business, publish your book, Peggy has the proven track record to help you achieve your goals.

To explore the ways in which Peggy can help you demand more of yourself and live your dreams, please visit:

{ **www.PeggyMcColl.com** }

For step-by-step guidance on creating your dream life using your own Power Life Script®, visit:

{ **www.PowerLifeScript.com** }